A Book for Christmas

Selma Lagerlöf (1858–1940) was a teacher in a girls' secondary school before she became a full-time writer. She is known around the world for her classic children's book *The Wonderful Adventure of Nils Holgersson* and she was the first female writer to win the Nobel Prize in 1909.

A Book for Christmas

And Other Stories

SELMA LAGERLÖF

*Translated by Sarah Death, Peter Graves
and Linda Schenck*

PENGUIN BOOKS

PENGUIN CLASSICS

UK | USA | Canada | Ireland | Australia
India | New Zealand | South Africa

Penguin Books is part of the Penguin Random House group of companies
whose addresses can be found at global.penguinrandomhouse.com.

This selection first published 2024
002

Cover: Detail from *In the Snow* (1910) by Carl Larsson. Watercolour
and pencil on paper. Private collection. Photo: Bridgeman Images

English translations © Sarah Death, Peter Graves, Linda Schenck, 2024

Set in 12.5/14.75pt Garamond MT Std
Typeset by Jouve (UK), Milton Keynes
Printed and bound in Great Britain by Clays Ltd, Elcograf S.p.A.

The authorized representative in the EEA is Penguin Random House Ireland,
Morrison Chambers, 32 Nassau Street, Dublin D02 YH68

A CIP catalogue record for this book is available from the British Library

ISBN: 978-0-241-71506-2

www.greenpenguin.co.uk

Contents

A Book for Christmas

A Memory from Childhood

We are sitting at the big drop-leaf table, one Christmas Eve at Mårbacka. Papa sits at one end of the table and Mama at the other.

Uncle Wachenfeldt is there – he is in the place of honour, on Papa's right-hand side – and Aunt Lovisa and Daniel and Anna and Gerda and I. Gerda and I sit where we always do, on either side of Mama, because we are the youngest. I can still see it all so clearly.

We have already had our traditional dinner of fish in white sauce, rice porridge and pastries. Plates, spoons, knives and forks have been cleared away, but the cloth is still on the table, two hand-dipped, branched candles are burning in their holders in the middle, and around them stand the salt cellar, the sugar pot, the cruet set and a big silver bowl, filled to the brim with Christmas beer.

With the meal being over, we really should get up from the table, but we do no such thing. We sit there waiting for the Christmas presents.

There is no other house in the district where they hand out the Christmas presents at the dinner table in the evening, after everyone has had their Christmas rice porridge. But it is an old custom at Mårbacka, and we like it that way.

There is nothing better than waiting hour after hour all through a long Christmas Eve and knowing that the best is still to come. The time passes slowly, very slowly, but we are convinced that other children, who had their Christmas presents at seven or eight in the morning, did not find it as pleasurable as we do now that the long-awaited moment has finally arrived.

Our eyes are glistening, our cheeks are aflame and our hands tremble as the door opens for the two housemaids, dressed up as traditional Christmas straw goats, to bring in a pair of big baskets, loaded with Christmas parcels, and drag them to Mama's seat.

Then Mama picks up one parcel after another, taking her time. She reads out the name of the recipient, deciphers the scrawled verses of dedication and hands round the gifts.

We are quite silent for those first moments as we wrestle with sealing wax and paper. But soon there is an outburst of happy exclamations. We talk and laugh and try to identify handwriting and compare our presents and do nothing to hide our delight.

On the specific Christmas Eve of which I am thinking, I have recently turned ten and I am sitting at the Christmas table in a state of utmost anticipation. I know so well, so very well, which present I would most like to receive. Not pretty dress fabrics or lace or brooches or ice skates or bags of sweets, but something else entirely. I do so hope that someone has had the idea of giving me a present of that kind!

The first Christmas present I unwrap is a sewing box and I know at once that it is from Mama. It has little compartments inside, and she has filled them with a sleeve of needles, some darning wool, a skein of black silk, wax and thread. Mama is no doubt reminding me that I should try to be a little more competent in my needlework and not think only of reading.

From Anna I get an excellent little embroidered pincushion that fits into another compartment of the box. From Aunt Lovisa there is a silver thimble and Gerda has sewn me a little sampler to help me mark my own stockings and handkerchiefs in the future.

Aline and Emma Laurell have gone back home to Karlstad, but they have left presents, for me and for all of us. Aline's gift is a little pair of embroidery scissors in a case that she has ingeniously made from a lobster claw and a piece of silk. From Emma I get a little hedgehog made of red wool, with pins for its spiky back instead of spines.

They are very nice and dainty, all these presents I have received, but I start to feel slightly uneasy. There are an awfully large number of sewing items here. What if I am not going to get the one thing that my heart desires?

For I must tell you about the special rule at Mårbacka that when we go to bed on Christmas night, we are allowed a table next to our beds with a candle on it, and then we can lie there and read for as long as we wish; that is the most exquisite of all Christmas pleasures. Nothing compares with lying back with a thrilling new book you have been given, a book you have never seen before, and which is a novelty to everybody else in the household too, and knowing you can go on reading page after page for as long as you are able to stay awake. But what shall I do on Christmas night if nobody has given me a book?

That is what I cannot help thinking as I open one parcel after another and find sewing accessories in all of them. I feel my ears going all hot; it's a blatant conspiracy. To think that I might not get a book for Christmas!

Daniel gives me a smart crochet hook made of bone, from Johan I get a dainty little winding card for leftover lengths of thread, and last of all, Papa comes over with a big present, an embroidery frame, which he has commissioned from the fine carpenter of Askersby. It is just like the ones his sisters used when they were growing up, he says.

'I expect you will be a real champion needlewoman, now that you have so many lovely sewing articles,' says Mama.

There are gales of laughter from the others. I imagine they can see from my face that I am not particularly pleased with my Christmas presents and they no doubt think they have played an especially good prank on me.

The gift distribution is nearly over and I have already had all the parcels I can hope for. I can expect nothing more.

Aunt Lovisa has got a novel and two Christmas almanacs, *Svea* and *Nornan*, and I will be able to enjoy those eventually, but Aunt must read them first. Oh dear, it is no easy matter to put a brave face on it and look happy.

When Mama picks the last parcel out of the present basket, I can see from the shape of it that it is a book. Of course, it is not for me. They have all conspired to agree that I am not to have a book.

But the parcel really is addressed to me, and when I have it in my hands, I can immediately tell that it is a book. I feel my face flush with joy and I positively shriek in my eagerness to borrow some scissors and cut the string. I tear off the paper at terrific speed and in front of me I see the most beautiful little book, a book of fairy tales. I can see that much from the pictures on the cover.

I can sense everybody at the table looking at me. They know, naturally, that this is my favourite Christmas present, the only one that I am really pleased with.

'What sort of book is it you've got?' says Daniel, leaning over me. I open it at the title page and just sit there staring. I do not understand a word.

'Let me see,' he says, and then he reads:

'*Nouveaux contes de fées pour les enfants par Mme la Comtesse de Ségur.*'

He shuts the book and hands it back to me. 'It's a book of fairy tales in French,' he says, 'so now you'll have something to keep you amused.'

I did a term of French with Aline Laurell, but when I take the book and glance through it, I cannot comprehend a word.

Being given a book in French is almost worse than

being given no book at all. It is very hard to hold back my tears. But luckily my eye is caught by an illustration on one page of the book.

It shows an enchanting little princess in a carriage drawn by two ostriches, and riding on the back of one of the ostriches is a pageboy in a plumed hat and a braided frock coat. The princess herself has big, puffed sleeves and flouncy ruffles at her neck. The ostriches have tall plumes of feathers on their heads and their bridle straps are broad gold chains. You could not wish to see anything prettier.

As I continue leafing through the book, I find a whole treasure trove of illustrations: pictures of proud princesses, splendid kings, noble knights, dazzling fairies, loathsome witches and wondrous fairy-tale palaces. It is certainly no book to shed tears over, even though it is in French.

All through Christmas night I lie there and look at the pictures, especially that first one with the ostriches. I find enough to entertain me for many hours.

On Christmas Day, after we have been to the early service at church, I take out a little French dictionary and start reading in French.

It is hard. My studies have been confined to Grönlund's method. If these fairy tales were to say things like 'the big man's little hat' or 'the good carpenter's green umbrella' then I would understand, but how am I to cope with an extended text in French?

The book of fairy tales starts like this: *Il y avait un roi.*

What does that mean? It takes a good hour for me to reach the point of understanding that this can be translated as: 'Once upon a time there was a king'.

But the pictures are enticing. I must know what they depict. I hazard guesses and I search the dictionary and I work my way through, line by line.

By the end of the Christmas holidays, that pretty little book has taught me more French than I would have picked up in years from Aline Laurell and Grönlund combined.

The Legend of Saint Lucia's Day

Many hundreds of years ago in the southern part of Värmland there lived a wealthy, miserly old woman known as Mistress Rangela. She owned a castle, or rather a fortified estate, at the narrow mouth of a long bay of Lake Vänern that extends deep into the countryside. Across the mouth of this bay she had a bridge constructed, which could be raised like the drawbridge over a moat. Mistress Rangela maintained a large contingent of guards at this bridge. For wayfarers prepared to pay her bridge toll, a guard quickly lowered the bridge, whereas for others who refused to pay, out of poverty or for any other reason, it remained up. Since there was no ferry, such travellers had no other option than to take a long detour of many extra miles to round the bay.

Mistress Rangela's trick of collecting a toll like this from wayfarers roused a great deal of indignation, and probably the defiant peasants who lived nearby would long ago have forced her to grant them free passage had she not had a powerful friend and protector, Lord Eskil of Börtsholm, whose property bordered on her own. This gentleman, Lord Eskil, lived in a true castle with both walls and turrets, and was so wealthy that his combined earthly possessions corresponded to an entire county. He rode the countryside accompanied by sixty armed men, and was a trusted advisor to the king. Not only was he a good friend of Mistress Rangela's, she had also contrived to make him her son-in-law, and under such circumstances it was perfectly natural for no one to dare provoke the greedy woman in her dealings.

Year after year Mistress Rangela continued her trade undisturbed, until something happened that threw her scheme into jeopardy. Her unfortunate daughter suddenly died, and Mistress Rangela was quick to realize that a man like Lord Eskil, with eight young children and a court comparable to a king's, would soon marry again, not least because he was far from aged. But if his new wife should take a dislike to Mistress Rangela there might be serious problems in the making. It was at least as important for her to be on a good footing with the mistress of Börtsholm as with the master, since Lord Eskil, who had many significant matters to deal with, was often away from home and when he was away it was up to his wife to organize and dictate over their home and property.

Mistress Rangela gave the matter a great deal of thought, and once the funeral had been held she rode over to Börtsholm one day and sought out Lord Eskil in his private chamber. She began the conversation by calling to mind his eight children and the care they required, his enormous staff of servants who needed to be overseen, fed and clothed, the huge banquets to which he never hesitated to invite kings and princes, his enormous income from his herds and his farmlands, his hunting woods, his beehives, his hop gardens, his fishing waters, all the crops from the castle farm which had to be conserved and prepared; in other words, everything his wife had always managed. Thus, she intended to provoke in him a great deal of anxiety about the tremendous difficulties he was facing now that his wife had passed on.

Lord Eskil listened with the respect a mother-in-law is due, as well as with a certain unease. He feared that the upshot of all this was to be that Mistress Rangela intended to offer to become his housekeeper at Börtsholm, and he said to himself that this old woman with her double chin and crooked nose, her deep voice and her peasant manners would not be what he considered pleasant company in his home.

'My dear Lord Eskil,' Mistress Rangela went on, probably not unaware of the effect her diatribe was having, 'I know that you will have every opportunity to make the most significant possible marriage, but I also know that you are sufficiently wealthy to think more of the welfare of your children than of a dowry and an inheritance, and for that reason I am now proposing to you to choose one of my daughter's young cousins to succeed her.'

Lord Eskil's face brightened visibly when he realized that it was a young relation his mother-in-law was proposing, and she continued to persuade him, with increasing confidence, to marry Lucia, the daughter of her brother Justice Sten Folkesson, who would be turning eighteen that winter, on Saint Lucia's Day. She had been raised by and lived with the pious sisters at Riseberga convent, who taught her good manners and a strict fear of God. She took part daily in the activities of the large convent household and had thus learned to manage a fine estate.

'Were it not for the obstacles of her youth and poverty,' said Mistress Rangela, 'she should be the woman of your choice. I believe it would have lightened the heart of my late daughter to know that her children would be raised by Lucia. If you make the cousin of your late wife their stepmother, my daughter will have no need to rise up from her grave to protect her children, as did Lady Dyrit of Örehus.'

Lord Eskil, who had little, if any, time to think about his own personal affairs, was deeply grateful to Mistress Rangela for suggesting such a suitable marriage. Although he did request a few weeks' time to think, it only took a couple of days for him to grant Mistress Rangela his authorization to negotiate on his behalf. And as quickly as could be done with consideration to the necessities, to the preparations and to decency, the wedding was held. And in the early spring, just a few months after her eighteenth birthday, his young wife took her place at Börtsholm.

When Mistress Rangela thought about the debt of gratitude owed her by her niece for having made her the fine lady of a prosperous, elegant castle, one might say that she felt even more secure than when her own daughter held sway there. In her joy, she raised the drawbridge charges by a few pennies and strictly forbade all the neighbours to help travellers to cross the bay by boat, so no one could get around paying the toll.

It came to pass one lovely day when Lady Lucia had been at Börtsholm for a few months that a group of pilgrims in ill health who were making their way to the spring of the Holy Trinity near the village of Sätra in Västmanland requested permission to cross the bridge. These people, on a pilgrimage to regain their well-being, were accustomed to those who lived along their route assisting them as best they could as they wandered, and more often than not giving them alms rather than expecting them to pay a toll. However, Mistress Rangela's guards were under strict orders not to display the slightest leniency, particularly towards pilgrims of this nature, whom she suspected of being in better health than they pretended to be and to be roaming the land out of pure indolence.

When the ailing pilgrims were denied free passage, there arose among them a wailing beyond compare. The lame and crippled pointed to their withered limbs, asking how anyone could be so cruel as to wish to extend their journey by a full day's travel, the blind fell to their knees on the road and tried to grope their way to the bridge guards to kiss their hands, while some of the friends and companions of the pilgrims, who were helping them along their way, turned their wallets and pouches inside out before the eyes of the guards to show them that they were truly empty.

The guards stood there, quite unyielding, and the poor souls were absolutely inconsolable when, to their good fortune, the lady of the castle at Börtsholm and her stepchildren came rowing along the bay. She hastened to see what the uproar was all about, and as soon as she understood the trouble she burst out:

'This is surely the easiest matter in the world to remedy. The children will simply go ashore for a while and visit with their grandmamma, Mistress Rangela, while I transport these ailing pilgrims across the bay in my boat.'

Both the guards and the children, who knew that Mistress Rangela was not a woman to be toyed with as regarded the drawbridge fees she held so dear, tried with facial expressions and gestures to warn the new Lady, but she either did not notice or did not wish to notice. For this woman was unlike her aunt, the brusque Mistress Rangela. Ever since earliest childhood Lady Lucia loved and respected the Sicilian virgin Lucia, her patron saint, and held her close to her heart as a model. In return, the saint had pervaded her entire being with light and warmth, notable even in her outward appearance. She stood shimmering and nearly transparent, so lovely that people almost feared to touch her.

With many kind words to the ailing pilgrims she transported them across the sound, and after the last of the band disembarked on the desired shore, they heaped so many blessings upon her that if such cargo were as heavy as it is valuable her boat would have sunk to the bottom before she made it back to her own shore.

Blessings and good wishes were also precisely what she required as from that day her aunt, Mistress Rangela, began to suspect that her niece would not be a source of support to her, and she bitterly regretted having made her the wife of Lord Eskil. She, who had so readily elevated her impoverished young niece, decided that before Lady Lucia could do her even more injury, she would pull her down from her high position and return her to her previous state of obscurity.

In order to come closer to her niece, she concealed her evil intentions for some time and paid her frequent visits at Börtsholm, where she did her very best to plant discord between the staff and their young mistress, so that she might tire of her situation. But to her vast astonishment she failed entirely in this project. This was most likely in part because, in spite of her youth, Lady Lucia knew how to keep her household in good order. But the real reason was surely that her children and her servants all seemed to be aware that their new mistress had some mighty heavenly protection, such that her foes were punished while all those who served her willingly and well received unexpected benefits.

Mistress Rangela soon understood that her strategy was doomed, yet she was not prepared to abandon hope until she also tried Lord Eskil. But he was at the royal court for most of the summer, involved in long and difficult negotiations. When he did occasionally come home for a day or two, he devoted most of his time to his various overseers and game wardens. He took very little notice of the women at Börtsholm, and even when Mistress Rangela came to visit he kept his distance, so she never managed to see him alone.

One lovely summer's day, when Lord Eskil was at

Börtsholm and sat in his private chamber conversing with his stable manager, the castle resounded with such loud screaming that he was forced to interrupt his conversation and rush out to discover the cause.

He found his mother-in-law, Mistress Rangela, upon her horse, outside the castle portal, shrieking louder than a horned owl.

'It is your unfortunate children, Lord Eskil,' she cried. 'They are in distress out on the lake! They rowed across to my shore this morning, but on their way home their boat must have taken in water. I could see from home what difficulty they were in, and so I rode here to alert you! I would add, despite your wife being my very own niece, that she made a very poor decision in allowing them to come across on their own in such an inadequate craft. To be honest it looks like just the kind of ruse a stepmother might deploy.'

With a few quick questions, Lord Eskil learned what he needed to know about the children's whereabouts and rushed down to the boat landing accompanied by his stable manager. But before they got very far they saw Lady Lucia and the entire band of children approaching along the steep path from the lake up to Börtsholm.

That day the young lady of the manor had not accompanied her children on their outing but stayed at home to attend to her duties. However, she seemed to receive a warning from her mighty heavenly protectress, because she suddenly left the castle to see how they were faring. She quickly caught sight of them waving and shouting, attempting to call for help from the shore, and rushed out to them in her own boat, and succeeded in the nick of time in transferring them to it from their own sinking craft.

When Lady Lucia and her stepchildren were coming up the walkway from the shore, she was so fully occupied with asking the children how they could have got into such distress, and they were so busy telling her, that they did not notice Lord Eskil coming towards them. Whereas he, who had become a shade suspicious due to Mistress Rangela's words about a stepmother's ruse, gestured quickly to his stable manager, and the two of them hid behind one of the big wild rose bushes that covered nearly the entire hillside on which Börtsholm castle stood.

From their hiding place, Lord Eskil heard the children explaining to Lady Lucia that they had left home in a fine boat, but during their visit to Mistress Rangela it had been changed for an old, flimsy one. They did not notice the switch until they were already out on the lake and the boat began to take in water from all directions, and they would surely have perished if their dear mother had not so speedily come to their rescue.

It seemed as if Lady Lucia had some idea of the real reason behind this change of boat, because standing there on the hillside she went deathly pale, tears came to her eyes and her hands moved to her heart. The children gathered around to comfort her, saying that after all they had survived unscathed, but she just stood there, powerless and immobile.

The two eldest of her stepchildren, young lads of fourteen or fifteen, held their hands in a square to make a little chair, on which they bore her triumphantly up the hill, with the younger ones behind them, laughing and clapping.

While this little band paraded up towards Börtsholm, Lord Eskil remained where he was, deep in thought, observing his wife and children. He seemed to find the young woman delightful and strangely radiant as she was borne past him, and he may very well have wished that, in spite of his age and his dignity, he could have taken her in his arms and carried her into the castle himself.

Perhaps, too, this was the moment when Lord Eskil realized how little pleasure he gained from all the effort he invested in the service of the great monarch, while peace and joy apparently attended him here at his very own hearth and home. At least for the remainder of that day he did not close himself up in his private chamber but spent his time speaking with his wife and watching his children at play.

Mistress Rangela, in contrast, saw all this with great displeasure, and hurried away from Börtsholm as quickly as decency allowed. But since no one seriously dared to suspect of her having jeopardized the lives of her grandchildren in order to bring disgrace upon Lady Lucia in the eyes of her lord and master, their friendly relationship was not disturbed, and she was able to go on as before doing what she could to deprive the young lady of the castle of her high position.

All the old woman's efforts appeared to be failing for

quite some time since Lady Lucia's kind heart and impeccable behaviour along with the help she received from her patron saint continued to make her unassailable to any and all attacks. But late that autumn, to the great satisfaction of Mistress Rangela, her niece embarked upon a project of which Lord Eskil could hardly fail to disapprove.

That year the harvest at Börtsholm was so bountiful that it surpassed the previous year, and in fact of all previous years for as far back as anyone could recall. The hunting and fishing too had proven to be more than twice as successful as usual. The beehives were overflowing with honey and wax, and the hop gardens with hops. The cows provided an abundance of milk, the sheep's wool grew as thick as grass, and the pigs' feed made them so fat they could barely move. This blessing was notable to everyone living at the castle, and they were quick to claim that it was thanks to their young mistress, Lady Lucia, that such prosperity had rained down upon them.

But while everyone at Börtsholm was now busily occupied with the work of conserving and preparing all the riches of the year's harvest, a large number of people in distress arrived, all from the eastern or northeastern shore on the opposite side of their large lake, Vänern. Weeping and wailing and gesturing pitifully, they described having been attacked by enemy troops who laid waste to their entire region, setting fires, plundering and murdering. These soldiers were so vicious that they even set fire to the grain and drove the livestock with them when they continued on. The people whose lives were spared were now facing a winter with neither food nor shelter. Some took to the roads as beggars, others holed up in the woods, others still wandered the burned-down homesteads, unable to set to work, simply grieving their losses.

When Lady Lucia heard the tales of their suffering, she became tormented by the sight of all the foodstuffs now accumulating at Börtsholm. Gradually the thought of the starving hordes on the opposite side of the lake overwhelmed her so that she could hardly put a morsel to her lips.

Every day she would think about the parables she had heard at the convent about holy men and women who sacrificed every stitch of their own clothing to help those who lived in poverty and misery. And above all she recalled the way in which her own patron saint, the holy Lucia of Syracuse, extended such mercy to a heathen youth who fell in love with her because of her beautiful eyes, that she drew her own eyeballs out of their sockets and gave them to him, bleeding and sightless, in order to cure him of his love for her, since she was a Christian virgin and could never be his. The young lady of the castle worried and suffered greatly over these memories and felt dreadful self-contempt for having let herself hear of all this misfortune without making any serious attempt to rectify it.

At the same time as she was agonizing over these thoughts, she received word from Lord Eskil that he was going to have to journey to Norway at the behest of the king, so she was not to expect him home before Christmas. But when he did arrive, he would be accompanied not only by his own sixty men but also by a large contingent of friends and companions, for which reason he requested that Lady Lucia prepare the castle for a great, prolonged banquet.

On the same day Lady Lucia was informed that her husband would not be returning during the autumn, she set about stilling the anguish that had been plaguing her for so long. She commanded her people to carry down to the shore all the prepared foodstuffs they had accumulated at Börtsholm. All the winter produce from the castle was loaded onto barges and ships, undoubtedly to the astonishment of the castle inhabitants.

When the cellars and attics were emptied, Lady Lucia, in the company of her children and her housemaids and servants, boarded fully loaded vessels and, leaving behind at Börtsholm only a small number of elderly guards to look after the castle, her party and all their effects rowed out onto the vast lake which lay before her, shoreless as an ocean.

There are many old tales and records of the voyage of Lady Lucia. For instance it is said that when she arrived at the opposite shore of Lake Vänern, the area to which the enemy had most thoroughly laid waste, it was virtually abandoned by its inhabitants. Lady Lucia, quite dejected, gazed ashore for signs of life and movement, but there was no smoke rising, no cock crowing, no cow mooing.

In one parish, there was an elderly minister by the name of Father Kolbjörn, who remained. He did not feel he could leave with his parishioners when they fled from their devastated homes, because both his parsonage and his church were filled with people wounded in the struggle. He stayed with them, tended their wounds and shared the little he possessed, allowing himself neither food nor rest. This resulted in such exhaustion that he felt his days were numbered. And then, on one of the darkest days of autumn, when heavy clouds filled the sky right down to the lakeshore, when the water rushed in with its black waves, and the grimness of nature compounded his despair and misery, poor Father Kolbjörn, who was no longer capable of reading a mass, tried to pull the rope of the church bell to call the blessings of God upon his ailing patients. And lo and behold, barely had the first bell pealed when a small fleet of little vessels and barges came rowing towards shore. And out of one of these ships a lovely young woman stepped ashore with a face glowing with light. Before her walked eight wonderful children, and behind her followed a long line of servants carrying all kinds of food: roast calves and sheep, long rods with cakes of dried bread, barrels of drink and sacks of flour. As if by a miracle, help had arrived in an hour of need.

Not far from Father Kolbjörn's church on a tongue of land known as Saxudden Point that extended sharply out into the lake, there had long been an ancient farm. It was burned down and plundered, but its owner, a seventy-year-old man, loved his homestead so deeply that he was unable to leave. His elderly wife stayed with him, along with a grandson and a granddaughter. They lived for some time on what fish they could catch, but one night a storm destroyed their nets and tackle, and since then they had sat among the ruins awaiting death by starvation. As they bided their time, the farmer pondered their dog, who lay there patiently with them, famished. The farmer grasped a stick and, mustering his old energy, struck out at the dog to drive him off, as he did not want the animal to die through no fault of its own. After being struck, the dog simply barked loudly and moved away. All night he prowled around the farmyard, howling incessantly. And the howling was heard on the lake, so that before daylight Lady Lucia, alerted by the barking, rowed to land and to their aid.

Even further off there was a little walled-in building, the home of a number of holy sisters who had vowed to God that they would never abandon their convent. The warriors showed sufficient consideration of these pious women that they harmed neither them nor their building, but they did take with them all their winter supplies. All they left was a dovecote full of doves, which the nuns killed one at a time until there was only one left. This dove was a very tame one, and the sisters loved it so dearly that they did not wish to extend their own lives by eating it, so they opened its cage and released it to liberty. The white dove rose high into the sky at first and then settled on the ridge of the roof. When Lady Lucia rowed past along the shore, gazing out for anyone requiring assistance, she saw the dove and knew that where there was a dove there must still be people. And so she went ashore and gave to the pious sisters all the food that they would need to survive the winter.

Even further south along the shore of Lake Vänern, there had been a small centre of commerce which was now both plundered and burned. Nothing but the long piers at which the ships docked in the old days remained. Here, under a jetty, during the time of destruction a man known as Lasse the tradesman hid with his wife who, while the tumult of battle was raging over their heads, had given birth to a child. Since then she had been so extremely ill that she was unable to flee, and her husband had stayed with her. Now they were in utter misery, and every day the woman pleaded with her husband to consider his own well-being and abandon her, but he could not do so, and refused. One night she tried to leave their hiding place taking the child with her to drown in the lake, thinking that if the two of them were dead her husband would leave and save his own life. But the child gave a loud cry in the cold water, and the husband awakened. He got them back up onto dry land, but the child was so terrified it wailed all night. And the sound carried across the water and brought them the ready and willing helpers from the lake, who had been watching and waiting.

For as long as she had gifts left to give, Lady Lucia travelled the coast of Lake Vänern, and during this journey she was as happy and light-hearted as she had ever been. Because just as there is nothing more burdensome than sitting still doing nothing when we hear of the terrible misfortunes of others, there is nothing more heartwarming or calming for anyone than doing whatever small things we can to mitigate them. She was still feeling this kind of relief and pleasure, without a thought that anything awful might befall her, when she returned to Börtsholm quite late on the eve of Saint Lucia's Day. At their supper, which consisted only of a few mugs of milk, she spoke with her travelling companions of the fine journey they had made, and there was general consensus that none of them had ever passed more joyous days.

'But now we have hard work ahead of us,' she continued. 'Tomorrow we will not be able to celebrate Saint Lucia's Day eating and drinking as we have in the past. We must get down to brewing and butchering and baking, and we will have to continue straight through if we are to have the Christmas fare ready for the return of Lord Eskil.'

The young lady said this without the least anxiety, because she knew that her livestock barns and grain larders and storehouses were filled with God's good gifts, although for the moment, none of it was ready to be eaten.

Because all the participants were quite exhausted they retired to their beds at an early hour, despite the success of their journey. Yet hardly had Lady Lucia shut her eyes when the pounding of horses' hooves could be heard outside the castle walls, as well as the rattle of weapons, and loud shouting. The creaking of the castle portal on its hinges was heard, followed by the trampling of eager boots on the cobblestones in the courtyard. She realized that Lord Eskil must have returned with his troops.

Lady Lucia quickly leapt from bed to receive him. Having hastily straightened her clothing she hurried out onto the landing on her way to the stairs to the castle courtyard. She got no further than the top step before she saw Lord Eskil already on his way up to their chamber.

He was preceded by a torchbearer, and it was clear to Lady Lucia in the torchlight that her husband's features were horribly distorted with anger. For an instant she told herself that it was the red, smoke-charred light from the torch that made his face appear so dark and threatening, but when she saw how pitifully her children and servants were looking, eyes lowered as they made way for him, she had to admit to herself that her husband had returned enraged and prepared to judge her and mete out punishments.

At the moment Lady Lucia stood there looking down at Lord Eskil, he, too, looked up at her, and she noted with increasing concern that his face took on a forced grimace.

'Do you approach, my gracious wife, to offer me a welcoming meal?' he asked facetiously. 'Well, at this moment your kindly trouble is in vain, as my men and I have had our evening meal at the home of your aunt, Mistress Rangela. Tomorrow, however,' he added, at which point his fury so possessed him that he pounded the banister, 'we expect you, in honour of your patron Saint Lucia, to serve us a breakfast of the castle's very finest fare, nor shall you neglect to bring me my morning beverage at the first crowing of the cock.'

The young lady was unable to utter a single word. In the same way as the previous summer, when she had sensed for the first time that Mistress Rangela harboured evil intent towards her, she simply stood there, with her hands to her heart and tears in her eyes. She could hardly think there was any other explanation than that Mistress Rangela had called Lord Eskil home at precisely the worst moment, and then precipitated his anger by telling him what liberties Lady Lucia had been taking with his possessions.

But Lord Eskil continued up a few steps and, without being the least bit moved by his wife's anxiety, bent towards her and said, in a terrifying voice:

'I vow on the cross of our Saviour, Lady Lucia, that if breakfast is not to my satisfaction, you will regret it for the rest of your life. Mark my words.'

Having said that, he laid his hand heavily upon his wife's shoulder and urged her ahead of him in the direction of the bedchamber.

As they walked towards the chamber, Lady Lucia felt that something which was previously strangely unclear to her became suddenly apparent. She realized that she had behaved wilfully and thoughtlessly, and Lord Eskil probably had very good reason to be furious with her for having made arbitrary use of his resources without consulting him. And she tried, once they were alone together, to express her regret to him for her actions and beg him to forgive her for her youthful imprudence, but he never gave her the opportunity.

'Now get yourself abed, Lady Lucia,' he told her, 'and do not so much as dare think of arising earlier than your normal hour! If my morning drink and welcoming meal do not meet with my satisfaction, I assure you that you will need all the energy you can muster, for you will have a long run ahead of you.'

She had no choice but to accept this statement, although it only increased her fears, and it is easy to imagine that no sleep came to her eyes that night. She lay there reminding herself of what her husband had said, and the more she considered his words, the clearer it became to her that they contained a powerful threat. He had surely set his mind to the idea that he did not want to pass judgement on her until he had seen with his own eyes that she had behaved as despicably as Mistress Rangela claimed. So if she proved to be unable to offer him the meal he had requested, then there was no doubt that a terrible punishment awaited her. At the very least she would be declared no longer fit to be his wife and be sent home to her parents, but his final words seemed to her to contain a further intention on his part to condemn her to run the gauntlet between lines of his soldiers like some simple thieving wench.

Now that she had fathomed the state of things, and they truly were as she thought, because Mistress Rangela had riled Lord Eskil up into a terrible rage, Lady Lucia began to tremble, and her teeth to chatter, and she felt as if her death were imminent. She knew that she ought to use the hours of the night to seek succour and solutions, but her overwhelming fear paralysed her to the degree that she simply lay there, immobile. 'How can I possibly provide a meal for my Lord and his sixty troops tomorrow morning?' she asked herself in despair. 'I may just as well lie still and wait for misfortune to strike.'

The only thing she managed to do for her own salvation was to send powerful prayers, hour after hour, to Saint Lucia of Syracuse.

'Oh, Saint Lucia, my beloved patron mother,' she prayed, 'tomorrow is the day you suffered martyrdom and entered the heavenly gates. Call to mind the darkness and chill and difficulty of living on earth! Come to me tonight and transport me with you and away from here! Come and shut my eyes in the sleep of death! You know that this is my only recourse to allow me to escape ignominy and a shameful punishment.'

While she called for the aid of Saint Lucia, the night passed, and the morning she had dreaded grew closer. Far sooner than she anticipated, the first crowing of the cock was heard, the cattle herders crossed the courtyard to commence their daily chores, and the horses rose noisily in their boxes.

'Now Lord Eskil will also awaken,' she thought. 'He will surely soon command me to bring him his morning beverage, at which time I will have to admit that I have behaved so negligently that I have neither beer nor mead to warm for him.'

At this most perilous moment for the young lady of the castle her heavenly ally, Saint Lucia, who was surely aware that the only error her charge had committed was that of displaying charity to excess, was unable any longer to resist the urge to come to her rescue. The earthly body of the holy woman, which had rested for hundreds of years in the narrow tomb in the catacombs of Syracuse, was instantly filled with a living spirit, took on once again her beauty and possession of her limbs, dressed in apparel woven of starlight, and moved once more into the world where she had suffered and loved.

And just a few moments later the astonished guard in the portal tower at Börtsholm saw a nocturnal miracle, a ball of fire, appearing in the southernmost skies. It shot through space more rapidly than an eye could follow its course and, heading right towards Börtsholm, bypassed the guard so closely that it nearly touched him, and vanished. But on this ball of fire, at least as the guard perceived it, there rode a young woman who balanced on the tip of one toe, stretching her arms high, a playful, dancing passenger of the glowing vessel.

At almost the same instant poor, terrified Lady Lucia saw, in her anguish and her tense anticipation, a glow seeping through a crack in her bedchamber door. And a moment later when the door opened, to her astonishment and joy, a beautiful young woman entered the room, dressed in garments as white as starlight. In her long, black hair was a garland of greenery, made not of ordinary leaves and flowers but of a branch of tiny, blinking stars. These stars illuminated the entire chamber and yet, to Lady Lucia, this light was nothing compared with the eyes of this divine stranger, which not only shone clear and bright but also radiated heavenly love and charity.

This unknown young woman carried a large copper

jug from which came the delicate scent of the finest grape nectar, and she floated across the chamber bearing it to Lord Eskil. She poured him a small bowl of this wine and bade him drink.

Lord Eskil, having slept well, awoke when the shimmer of light struck his eyelids, and lifted the bowl to his lips. In his only semi-conscious state he barely experienced any more of the miracle than that the wine he was offered was delicious, and he drank the bowl to the dregs.

But this wine, which could hardly have been anything but the imperial Malvasia, the glory of the south and the noblest of all wines, was so soporific that the moment he set down the bowl he fell back onto the bed, sound asleep. And at that very moment the beautiful, holy virgin floated back out of the room, leaving Lady Lucia in a state of fearful wonder and newly aroused hope.

The shimmering attendant did not content herself with providing a morning drink for Lord Eskil alone. That dark, cold winter morning she made her way through all the gloomy rooms of that Swedish castle, offering each and every one of the sleeping soldiers a bowl of the splendid wine from the south.

Each person who drank came away with the impression that he had been offered a taste of blissful delight. Nor could they resist instantly falling back into a sleep filled with dreams of places where eternal summer and sunlight prevailed.

Lady Lucia, in turn, had barely lost sight of this bright apparition when the anguish and powerlessness that had plagued her all night dissipated entirely. She dressed in great haste, after which she summoned her household to work.

Throughout that long winter morning they all busied themselves preparing the welcome meal for Lord Eskil. Young calves, piglets, geese and hens were hastily slaughtered, dough was set to rise, fires were lit under the spits and in the ovens for baking, cabbage was browned, turnips were peeled and honey cakes were baked for the sweet course.

The tables in the banquet hall were covered with cloths, the finest beeswax candles unpacked from deep within chests, the benches covered with blue down bolsters and tapestries.

The lord of the castle and his men remained asleep throughout these preparations. When Lord Eskil finally arose, he could tell from the position of the sun that it was midday. He was surprised not only by his long sleep but possibly even more by having slept off the indignation that had plagued him the night before. During his morning dreams, his wife had appeared to him in great mildness and sweetness, and he was now astonished at himself, that he had been of a mind to sentence her to a harsh and shameful punishment.

'Things may not be as bad as Mistress Rangela has made me believe,' he thought to himself. 'Of course I will not be able to keep her as my wife if she has been misappropriating my possessions, but it may well suffice to send her back to her parents with no further punishment.'

When he left the bedchamber, he was greeted by his eight children, who guided him along to the banquet room. His men were already seated, waiting impatiently for him to arrive so they could devote themselves to eating, for the table in front of them was heaped with all kinds of lovely dishes.

Lady Lucia sat down at her husband's side with no sign of concern. But she was not freed from all her worries since, although she had managed to hastily prepare the food, she had absolutely no beer or mead to offer them, as such drinks take some time to mature. And she was quite uncertain as to whether Lord Eskil would consider himself well provided for at a breakfast without such beverages.

Then she noticed on the table in front of her the large copper jug the holy virgin had been carrying. There it stood, full to the brim with fragrant wine. Once again she was heartfully overjoyed with the protection of her merciful patron saint, and she offered Lord Eskil the wine, telling him how it had come to Börtsholm, while he listened in total amazement.

After Lord Eskil had taken a few sips of the wine which, this time, did not have a soporific effect but on the contrary only made the drinkers cheerful and refined, Lady Lucia once again gathered her courage and told him the tale of her journey. Initially, Lord Eskil sat still and grave, but when she got to the point when she encountered the minister, Father Kolbjörn, he burst out:

'Father Kolbjörn is a faithful friend of mine, Lady Lucia. It pleases my heart that you were able to help him.'

It also transpired that the farmer with the large holdings at Saxudden had accompanied Lord Eskil on many campaigns, that one of the pious nuns was an aunt of his, and that Lasse the town tradesman was the customary importer of his garments and weapons. Before Lady Lucia reached the end of her story, Lord Eskil was prepared not only to forgive her but also to be infinitely grateful to her for having aided so many of his friends.

Still, the anguish that Lady Lucia had suffered during the night reappeared once more, and there was weeping in her voice when she finally said:

'It does seem to me personally, my respected Lord, that I behaved very badly by having misappropriated your property without asking your permission. But I plead with you to take into account the fact that I am very young and inexperienced, and for that reason to forgive me.'

When Lady Lucia spoke these words and Lord Eskil pondered on his realization that his wife was such a pious woman that one of the inhabitants of Heaven had resumed her worldly apparition and come to her aid, and when he went on to consider the way in which he, who presumed to be a wise and discerning man, had been suspicious of her and prepared to vent his rage upon her, he felt so utterly mortified that he lowered his eyes and was unable to reply to her with one single word.

When Lady Lucia saw him sitting there silently, with his head bowed, she was again horrified, and would have liked more than anything to flee the room in tears. But then, unseen by all, the merciful Saint Lucia crept close to the young lady and whispered into her ear the words to say. And these words were precisely the ones Lady Lucia herself would have wished to pronounce but which, without this heavenly intervention, she would have been too timid ever to utter.

'There is one more request I would like to make of you, my respected Lord and master,' she said, 'and that is for you to dwell more often in our presence. Under such circumstances, I would never be tempted to violate your will, and it would allow me to show you all the love I feel for you, such that no one could force their way between the two of us.'

When she spoke these words, it was clear to one and all that they were greatly to the liking of Lord Eskil. He raised his head and his great joy banished all his mortification.

He was about to deliver the kindest possible reply to his wife when one of Mistress Rangela's deputies rushed into the banquet hall. He hastened to report that early that morning Mistress Rangela had been making her way to Börtsholm in order to attend the punishment of Lady Lucia. But she crossed paths with some peasants who had long detested her on account of the bridge toll and, encountering her in the dark accompanied by only a single servant, they first frightened him so much he fled, after which they pulled Mistress Rangela down from her horse and murdered her in cold blood.

Mistress Rangela's deputy was now out hunting down the murderers and requested of Lord Eskil that he also send out some of his men to assist in the search.

Lord Eskil rose up and spoke in a loud, stern voice:

'It seems as if the most suitable thing for me to do at the moment would be to reply to my wife's pleas, but before I do I must conclude on the matter of Mistress Rangela. And to that end I say, as far as I am concerned, let her lie there unavenged, and under no circumstances will I send out my servants to carry out murderous acts on account of her, because I have every reason to believe that her own misdeeds have proved her downfall.'

Having said this, he turned to Lady Lucia, and now his voice was so gentle it was difficult to believe that his throat could produce such tones.

'But to my dearest wife my response is that I gladly forgive her, as I hope she will excuse my hot temper. And as it is her wish, I shall request the king to select someone other than myself as his advisor, because I now wish to enter into the service of two noblewomen. One of these is my wife, the other the holy Saint Lucia of Syracuse, in whose honour I intend to set up altars in each and every church and chapel located on my lands, appealing to her that she keep alight the flame and lodestar known as charity that languishes in the soul of each of us who inhabit this cold, northerly clime.'

During my childhood, on the 13th of December each year, early in the morning when cold and darkness rule over us in the Värmland countryside, Saint Lucia of Syracuse still led her procession into every one of the widely scattered homes between the Norwegian mountains and the Gullspång River. She still came wearing, at least as she was perceived by the little children, a dress of white star-light, with a green wreath on her head in which candles blossomed brightly, and she still awakened the sleepers with a warm, fragrant drink from her copper jug.

Never in those days had I seen a more wondrous sight than when the door was opened and she entered the dark chamber. And surely I still hope that she will never cease to appear in the farmhouses of Värmland. For she is the light that dispels the darkness, she is the legend that van-quishes oblivion, she is the heartfelt warmth that makes the coldest parts of our world charming and radiant in midwinter.

The Princess of Babylon

It was a dark winter evening in the little cottage in Skro-lycka and Kattrinna, the woman of the house, was sitting spinning. The cat lay on her lap, purring along to the sound of the spinning wheel. Jan Andersson, her husband, was sitting by the stove, warming his back at the fire. He had been out the whole day cutting timber in Erik of Falla's forest, so no one could ask him to take on any more work now that he was at home. Even Kattrinna had nothing against him simply playing and chatting with their little girl, who was just five years old this winter.

Kattrinna sat there deep in her own thoughts and didn't listen to much of what her husband and child were talking about. There was one thing she was always strict about: she would not tolerate Jan telling the little girl that she was beautiful and special, as he was very fond of doing. For Kattrinna knew that if Klara Gulla were to form a high opinion of herself while she was still small, she would never become a sensible human being.

Jan was given to coming up with all sorts of things that might make the child conceited, but this evening Kat-trinna was quite untroubled because he was just telling her about things that had happened long ago, back when the earth was being created and humankind was beginning to people it. Just then he was telling her the story of the Tower of Babel and one could hope that this wouldn't give him a chance to come up with his usual silly ideas.

'Well, first they got hold of clay,' Jan said, 'and they made bricks and they slaked lime for mortar and they put up scaffolding and day by day the tower grew higher.

'They knew, of course, that building this tower was not pleasing to Our Lord, but they didn't let that concern them, as they had made up their minds to reach right up to Heaven so as to see what it looked like up there.

' "Now then, listen to me, my good people," Our Lord said. "I'm telling you this for the last time. If you don't leave this place and stop building, I shall really have to bring a catastrophe down upon your heads. And the catastrophe will be of such a kind that you will never be free from it and nothing will ever help you overcome it."

'But the people clearly thought that Our Lord would, as always, be patient with them and so they continued to build the tower and raised it higher with every passing day.

'And then Our Lord set to and confounded their language. Until that day, you see, they had all been able to understand one another, but now he put an end to that joy.

'Now when the master builders wanted to say "Bring me clay!", they said instead, "*Kolvipp, kolvapp!*" And when the apprentices asked what it was they were asking for, they would say, "*Erby, derby, mirby, marby?*" So, it's scarcely strange that they couldn't understand one another.

'The masters thought that the apprentices were mocking them, but when they wanted to say "Speak properly!", they said instead, "*Ullen, dullen, dorf!*" And when the apprentices wanted to know why they were looking so annoyed, they could do no more than utter "*Abracadabra?*"

'Now the masters and all the rest became so angry that they were soon at one another's throats and began fighting.

'From that day on, friendship between people was at an end and nobody wanted to build the tower anymore; instead they all went off their separate ways.'

When Jan had reached this point in his story, he glanced over at Kattrinna. The spinning wheel was silent and it almost looked as if both his wife and the cat had fallen asleep. So, Jan took up the story again, but he lowered his voice just a little.

'Now, among all those who had been there building the tower in Babylon there were also a king and a queen, who had a little princess. And, suddenly, this little girl also started speaking so strangely that neither her parents nor anyone else could understand a single word.

'The king and the queen no longer wanted to keep her at the castle with them and they drove her away, and she had to go out into the great, wide world all alone.

'She went and, of course, she was very unhappy. She didn't know who she might meet along the way. It would be an easy matter for bears and wolves to eat up such a little princess if they caught sight of her.

'But sweet and little as she was, no one did her any harm.

'No, on the contrary, everyone she met came up to her and greeted her and held out their hands and asked her where she was going. But since they couldn't understand a single word of her answer, they didn't bother about her anymore.

'Being as sweet and fine as she was, she only had to go up to castles and mansions and they all opened the doors wide to let her in. But no sooner had she opened her mouth and they heard the strange language she spoke than she had to be on her way again.

'At last, after passing through all the kingdoms there are, she arrived late one evening in a great forest, and when she emerged from this forest she caught sight of a tiny cottage. It was so low that she was only just able to go in through the door, but she went in and said, "Good evening!"

'There the little princess became so glad, because in that cottage they spoke a language she could understand. But she took great care not to tell them straightaway everything that had happened.

'"What's the name of this cottage?" she said, just to test them.

'"It's called Skrolycka," they answered at once, and she could see that they had understood her.

'She was now quite beside herself with joy, but she thought it best to test them one more time.

'"What's the name of the language you speak in this house?" she asked.

'"It's the language of Värmland," the people in the cottage answered.

'And, with that, the little princess went over to them and asked if she could stay there with them, because this was the only place in the world where people could understand what she was saying.

'But when she approached the fire, the people saw at once that she was a wee princess of Babylon and they said to her she was in quite the wrong place. And they told her there was no way she could feel at home with them but, they said, the language of Värmland was known on every farm in the neighbouring district and she would be able to settle wherever she pleased.

'But the little princess was not willing to give in. "No," she said, "I can see I'm in the right place. This is where I want to stay, because I can be both useful and bring joy."'

Little Klara Gulla had been sitting quite still in Jan's lap, her eyes growing wider and wider in astonishment as she listened. But now, as Jan finished the story, she sat utterly silent at first, then moved and turned her head to look at everything in the cottage as if she had never seen it before.

'Well, everything can stay as it is for a little while longer,' she said at last. 'But when I grow up, I'll no doubt go back to the place I came from.'

Jan's face fell, but the worst thing was that Kattrinna was awake now and had heard the last bit of their conversation.

'It just serves you right for forever making the little one fancy she is a grand lady!' she said.

The Rat Trap

Once upon a time a man selling small wire rat traps wandered the countryside. He made these traps himself in his idle moments, with materials he wheedled off the owners of general stores or large estates. Nonetheless his business wasn't very profitable and he had to resort to both begging and petty thievery to make ends meet. His clothing hung in rags from his body, his cheeks were sunken and his eyes radiated hunger.

One cannot even imagine how tedious and monotonous everyday life can be for such a peddler, who walks the roads with no company other than his own thoughts. But on this particular day this man found himself occupied with a chain of thought he felt was truly entertaining. He had been walking along thinking of his rat traps when it struck him that the entire world around him, the entire world with its countries and seas, cities and villages, was no more than one huge rat trap. The only reason it existed was to lure people into its trap: it offered them wealth and pleasures, shelter and food, heat and clothing all in the same way a rat trap offered cheese and pork, and the moment anyone allowed themself to be lured into touching the bait, it clamped down, and that was that.

The world had not treated him kindly, and so it gave him great pleasure to think badly of it in this way. He was well occupied during long, dull wanderings with thinking of people he knew who had let themselves fall into this dangerous trap, and of others who were still tiptoeing around the enticing bait.

As he trudged along one dark evening, he saw a little grey hut at the roadside and knocked at the door to request a night's lodging. And it was not denied him. Instead of the surly grimaces that often met him, the owner of this hut, an old man with neither wife nor children, was pleased to have someone to chat with in his solitude. After a few minutes he warmed the porridge pot over the fire and served some supper. Then he cut off a large enough chunk of tobacco from his twist that it was quite sufficient both for the stranger's pipe and his own. And then he pulled out a battered deck of cards, with which he and his guest played switch until bedtime.

The old man was just as generous with his confidences as with his porridge and tobacco. He quickly told his guest that when he was young and strong he had been a crofter at the iron mill at Ramsjö and a dayworker up at the manor. Nowadays, as he could no longer do daywork, his cow was his source of income. Indeed, she was a remarkable cow. She produced enough milk that he could sell some to the dairy every day. In fact, over the past month he had been paid the astonishing sum of thirty kronor.

The stranger must have looked sceptical, because the old man stood up and walked over to the window, took down a leather pouch from its nail in the window frame, and removed three rumpled ten-kronor notes. He held them up to the eyes of his guest, nodded importantly and replaced them in the pouch.

The next day both men were up early. The crofter was in a hurry to milk his cow, and the other man probably didn't feel it was right to lie abed once the old fellow was up. They left the hut together. The crofter locked the door and placed the key in his pocket. The rat trap man thanked him and bade him farewell, after which they went their separate ways.

But half an hour later the rat trap peddler was back at the house. He didn't try the door, just went straight to the window, broke a pane of glass, stuck in his hand and snatched the pouch with the thirty kronor. He took the money and put it in his own pocket. Then he hung the leather pouch right back where it belonged and went on his way.

As he continued along with the money in his pocket, he was feeling quite pleased with his cunning. He knew, of course, that he didn't dare walk on the road for a while but would have to turn off into the woods. For the first few hours this posed him no difficulties. Later in the day things got worse, as the forest in which he walked was a big, bewildering one. He did try to keep going in the same direction, but the paths wound and twisted so strangely, round and round. He walked and walked but never got to the far edge of the woods, and in the end he began to realize that he must have been walking in circles.

Just a moment later he recalled his thoughts about the world and the rat trap. Now it was his turn. He had let himself be enticed by the bait and he was caught. The whole forest, with its trunks and branches, undergrowth and trees brought down by the wind, surrounded him like an impenetrable prison where he was lost for ever.

It was late December, and night had already begun to descend on the forest. This increased the danger, as well as his dejection and desperation. In the end he did not know what to do, and sank to the ground exhausted, thinking his final hours had come.

At the very moment he lay down his head, though, he heard a sound. It was a hard, regular beating. There was no mistaking that noise. He sat up. 'That hammering comes from an iron mill,' he thought. 'There must be people nearby.' He mustered the last of his energy, rose up and staggered on in the direction of the noise.

2.

Not so long ago, Ramsjö's iron foundry, which has since closed down, was a large iron mill, with smelt works, rolling bars and forges. During the summer long lines of heavily loaded barges and cargo vessels sailed down the canal that led into a large lake, and in winter the roads around the mill were black with all the cinders sifting down from the huge iron wagons.

During one of these long, dark nights leading up to Christmas the master smith and his assistant were sitting by the blast furnace in the dark smithy waiting for the pig iron in the forge to be ready for the anvil. Time after time one of them would rise up to stir the white-hot mass with a long iron rod. A moment later he would turn back, dripping with sweat, although, true to custom, all he had on was a long shirt and clogs.

The smithy was constantly clamorous. The big bellows squeaked, the burning fuel crackled. The coal lad shovelled the coal noisily and it rattled into the gaping furnace. Outside, the rapids roared and a gusty northerly wind caused the rain to beat down on the roof tiles.

It was probably all this noise that prevented the smiths from noticing a man who had opened the door and entered the smithy, until he was standing right at the hearth.

It was surely not unusual, though, for poor drifters who had no better night's lodging to be attracted to the smithy by the sheen of light that filtered through the sooty window-panes, and who would come in to warm themselves by the fire. The smiths glanced only briefly and indifferently at the man who entered. He looked like people of his kind usually did. He had a long beard, was dirty and tattered, and had a bunch of rat traps dangling from his chest.

He asked whether he might stay, and the master smith nodded highly condescendingly, without so much as a word.

Neither did the vagabond speak. He had not come for a chat but only to be able to warm himself and get some sleep.

In those days Ramsjö mill had a very prominent owner, whose highest ambition was to supply the best-quality iron. Day and night, he monitored the work, ensuring that it was done as well as possible, and so he just happened to enter the smithy on one of his night vigils.

The first thing he saw was the tall, ragged fellow who was so close to the fire that his wet tatters were steaming. As opposed to the smiths, who had barely given the stranger a glance, the mill owner went close to him, inspected his appearance, and brusquely removed his floppy hat to get a closer look at his face.

'Well, if it isn't you, Nils Olof!' he said. 'What has become of you?'

The man with the rat traps had never before seen the mill owner from Ramsjö. In fact, he didn't even know his name. But he thought that if this fine gentleman believed he was an old acquaintance he might toss him a few kronor. He was in no hurry to alert him to his mistake.

'Well, God knows I have seen better days,' he replied.

'You ought never have agreed to be released from the regiment,' said the mill owner. 'That was where you went wrong. Had I still been there, I would never have let it happen. But now, needless to say, you must come along home with me.'

The thought of going up to the manor house to be received by the mill owner as an old regimental comrade did not appeal to the drifter.

'Dear Lord, no!' he said, looking quite horrified.

He was thinking about the thirty kronor. Going up to the manor would be like jumping into the lion's den. All he wanted was to sleep here in the smithy and then sneak off, drawing as little attention to himself as possible.

The mill owner assumed he was feeling ashamed of his miserable appearance.

'You mustn't think I have such a fine home that you cannot show yourself there,' he said. 'Elisabet has passed, as you may have heard. My lads are abroad, there is no one at home but my eldest daughter and me. We were just saying that it feels very dull not to have a single Christmas guest. Come along with me now and help us make a dent in all the Christmas fare.'

But the stranger said no and no and once again no, and the mill owner realized he was going to have to give up.

'All right, apparently Captain von Ståhle would rather spend the night here with you, Stjernström,' he said to the master smith, and turned on his heel.

He chuckled to himself as he was leaving and the smiths, who knew him, were very well aware that the final word had not yet been said.

And yes, less than half an hour later, the sound of carriage wheels could be heard outside the smithy, and another visitor came inside. It was not the proprietor returning. He had sent his daughter, clearly hoping that she would have greater powers of persuasion than he had.

She entered accompanied by a porter carrying a heavy fur in his arms. She was anything but beautiful and had quite a bashful appearance. In the smithy everything was as it had been earlier that night. The master smith and his assistant were still sitting on their bench, and the iron and coal were aglow in the forge. The stranger had stretched out on the floor and lay there with a bit of pig iron under his head and his hat pulled down over his eyes. As soon as the young woman saw him she walked over and lifted his hat. The fellow was apparently accustomed to sleeping with one eye open. He jumped straight up looking as if he had had a terrible fright.

'My name is Edla Willmansson,' said the young woman. 'When my father came home and told me that you, Captain, preferred to spend the night here in the smithy, I asked him to allow me to come down and collect you in the carriage and bring you home. I'm ever so sorry to see you in such dire straits, Captain.'

Looking at him with pity in her heavy eyes it struck her that the gentleman was frightened. 'He must either have stolen something or have escaped from prison,' she thought, and added quickly: 'You may rest assured, Captain, that we shall allow you to leave us just as freely as you have arrived. But please do spend Christmas Eve with us!'

She spoke these words most kindly, and the rat trap peddler must have felt that he could trust her.

'Never did I imagine, Miss, that you might personally go to such trouble,' he said. 'I shall come with you at once.'

He accepted the fur the porter extended to him with a deep bow, threw it across his shoulders over his ragged clothing, and followed the young lady out to the carriage without so much as a passing glance in the direction of the astonished smiths.

Yet it was with a sense of foreboding that he went along to the manor house. 'Damnation on me,' he thought to himself, 'for taking that man's money. Now I am caught in the trap and will never, ever get out.'

3.

The next day was Christmas Eve, and when the mill owner came into the dining room for breakfast he thought with pleasure of his old regimental comrade who had re-appeared so unexpectedly.

'Now first and foremost we must see to it to put a little meat on those bones of his,' he said to his daughter, who was busying herself by the table. 'And then I shall ensure that he has some other occupation than scurrying all over the country selling rat traps.'

'It surprises me that he has fallen so low,' said his daughter. 'Yesterday I didn't see a single indication that he once was an accomplished gentleman.'

'You'll have to have some forbearance, my dear girl,' said her father. 'As soon as we've got him properly cleaned up and dressed, you'll see he's a different man. He was, of course, ashamed of himself yesterday. His vagrant's manners will fall away when he's out of his vagrant's suit.'

Just as the mill owner said these words, the door opened

and the stranger entered. Yes, indeed, he was certainly properly cleaned up and dressed. The servant had bathed him, cut his hair and shaved his beard. And he was also wearing a nice everyday suit of the mill owner's, a white shirt with a starched collar, and a decent pair of shoes.

But in spite of the improvement in his guest's appearance, the mill owner did not look pleased. His brow furrowed as he considered him, and it became clear that when he saw the stranger in the fluttering light of the smithy hearth it had been easy for him to make a mistake, whereas now, with his guest standing there in broad daylight, there was no way he could take him for an old acquaintance.

'What on earth is this?' he thundered.

The stranger made no effort to dissemble. He could instantly see that the game was up.

'I am not at fault, Sir,' he said. 'I never pretended to be anything but a poor peddler, and I pleaded and begged to be left in the smithy. Nor is there any harm done. All I need do is to put my rags back on and be on my way.'

'Ah, well,' said the mill owner reluctantly. 'I cannot say, and you'll have to agree, that you played with an entirely open hand. Neither would I be surprised if the sheriff weren't interested in having a say about all this.'

The vagabond stepped forward and pounded his fist on the tabletop. 'Now, Sir, I shall tell you how it is. Life in this world is nothing but one big rat trap. Every tasty morsel on offer is nothing but cheese rinds and bits of pork set out to bring a poor fellow to ruin. And if the sheriff comes and puts me away for this, Sir, I'd ask you to consider that one day you yourself may be tempted to grab a juicy morsel of pork and find yourself caught in the trap.'

The mill owner began to laugh.

'I must admit you put that quite well, you did. I dare say we ought not to bother the sheriff on Christmas Eve. But be off with you now, as quick as you can!'

But just as the vagrant opened the door, the mill owner's daughter said, 'I think he ought to spend the day with us today. I don't want him to leave.' And she walked right over and shut the door.

'What in heaven's name do you think you're doing?' her father asked.

His daughter stood there, quite embarrassed, and not really knowing how to reply. That morning she had been feeling happy, thinking about what a nice Christmassy day she was going to arrange for that poor, famished fellow. She found it impossible to change her point of view so rapidly, which was why she had intervened on behalf of the drifter.

'My thoughts are with this poor stranger,' the young woman said. 'He walks the roads day in and day out, and there is probably not a single place in this entire land where he is welcome and can have a rest. Wherever he turns, they chase him off. He is constantly afraid of being arrested and interrogated. I would very much like us to give him a day of peace here at the manor, one single day out of the entire year.'

The mill owner mumbled a few words into his beard. He could find no way of opposing her.

'The whole incident was a mistake,' she went on, 'and yet I cannot find it in my heart to show the door to a man we have invited in with a promise of a merry Christmas.'

'You're sermonizing worse than a minister,' said the mill owner. 'Let us now hope you will not have cause to regret your words.'

The young woman took the stranger by the hand and led him to the table.

'Do sit down and eat now,' she said, understanding that her father had yielded.

The rat trap peddler said not a word, simply sat down and helped himself to something to eat. Time after time he gazed at the young woman who had interceded on his behalf. Why had she done so? What kind of yarn was being spun here?

That Christmas Eve at Ramsjö evolved more or less in the usual fashion. The stranger was not much trouble, as he slept most of the time. He lay on the divan in one of the guest rooms all morning, fast asleep. They woke him at lunchtime so that he could partake of all the delicious Christmas fare. But after lunch he went back to sleep. It was as if he had not been able to sleep so safely and calmly in many years as here at the mill at Ramsjö.

That evening when the Christmas tree was lit he was awakened again. He stood for a few minutes in the drawing room, blinking as if the candlelight was painful to his eyes. But then he was gone again. He was awakened once more two hours later to go down to the dining room for fish and rice porridge.

The moment they rose from the table, he went around to each person to say thank you and good night. When he came to the young woman, she informed him that her father had expressed his intention of giving him the suit of clothing he was wearing as a Christmas gift. He need not return it. And should he feel moved to spend next Christmas Eve somewhere where he could have a peaceful night's sleep and feel confident that no evil would befall him, he was welcome to return.

The rat trap peddler made no reply to these words. He merely stared at the young woman in utter astonishment.

The next morning the mill owner and his daughter rose in good time to make their way to the early service. Their guest was still asleep and they let him sleep on.

On their way home from church around ten o'clock the young woman sat hanging her head even more dejectedly than usual. She had heard in church that one of the old crofters from the estate had been robbed by a man who went around peddling rat traps.

'Goodness, that was some fine fellow you let into our house,' said her father. 'I can't help but wonder how many of our silver spoons are still in the cupboard.'

The carriage had barely stopped at the entrance when the mill owner asked his porter if the stranger was still there, adding that he had heard in church that the fellow was a thief. The porter replied that the man had left and that he certainly had not taken anything with him. On the contrary, he had left a little package which he hoped Miss Willmansson would accept as a Christmas present.

The young woman opened the packet, which was so badly wrapped that the contents quickly became visible, and gave a cry of delight. Enclosed was a little rat trap with three rumpled ten kronor notes stuck in it. Not only was the money all there, the trap also contained a note written in a large, awkward hand:

Respekted and grashus Miss.

Being as ya have showed kindness to me just as if I coulda been a Kaptin, I'd liketa show kindness back at ya just as if I was a reel Kaptin, cos I don' want ya to have the shaim of your Chrissmis vister being a robbur. So pleze return the money to the old geeza by the roadside whos got his cash pouch hangin from the winderframe as bate to temp a poor wandrer.

This here rat trap is fer Chrissmis from a rat that woudda been caught in the trap of the world if you adn't razed 'im up to a Kaptin, and that gived 'im the strenth to go on.

Sinin' with frendship and grate respekt

Kaptin from Stole.

In Nazareth

Once, when Jesus was only five years old, he was sitting on the step outside his father's workshop in Nazareth, busily moulding birds from a lump of clay he'd been given by the potter across the street. He was happier than he'd ever been because the local children had all told him that the potter was a mean man, who couldn't be moved either by sweet glances or by honeyed words, and so Jesus had never dared ask for anything from him. But now – and he scarcely knew how it had happened – he'd been standing there on the steps longingly watching his neighbour working with his moulds, when the potter came out of his shop and gave him clay – enough to make a wine flask.

Sitting on the steps outside the next house was Judas, who was red-haired and ugly, his face covered with bruises and his clothes all torn from the fights he was always getting into with street boys. For the moment he was at peace, neither teasing nor fighting but working with a lump of clay in the same way as Jesus. This wasn't clay he'd managed to get hold of for himself; he hardly dared let the potter catch sight of him as the man accused him of throwing stones at his fragile wares and would have driven him away with his cane. No, Jesus had shared his clay with him.

When the two children had finished their clay birds,

they lined them up in a circle in front of them. They looked just as clay birds have always looked throughout the ages, with big, round lumps to stand on instead of feet, short bodies, no necks and barely perceptible wings.

But there was an immediately visible difference between the work of the two little friends. Judas's birds were so lopsided that they invariably toppled over and however much he worked with his small, hard fingers, he could not make their bodies neat and well-formed. He stole glances over in the direction of Jesus to see what he was doing to make his birds as smooth and even as the oak leaves in the forests of Mount Tabor.

With every bird he finished, Jesus grew happier and happier. Each in turn seemed more beautiful than the one before and he studied them all with pride and love. They were to be his playmates, his little brothers and sisters; they would sleep in his bed, keep him company, sing their songs to him when his mother left him. Never before had he felt so rich, and never again would he need to feel lonely or deserted.

The big, burly water carrier walked past, bent under the weight of his heavy bag, and immediately behind him came the greengrocer, balancing on his donkey's back among big, empty wicker baskets. The water carrier laid his hand on Jesus's head and asked him about his birds, and Jesus told him that they all had names and that they could sing. All of his little birds had come to him from foreign countries and told him things that only he and they knew. Jesus spoke in such a way that both the water carrier and the greengrocer forgot their work for a long time in order to listen to him.

But when it came time for them to move on, Jesus pointed to Judas and said: 'Look at the beautiful birds Judas is making.'

The greengrocer was kind enough to rein in his donkey and ask Judas whether his birds, too, had names and could sing, but Judas would have none of it. He stayed stubbornly silent, not even looking up from his work, and at this the greengrocer kicked out angrily at one of the birds before riding on.

And so the afternoon passed, the sun sinking so far that its rays shone in through the low town gate that stood, crowned with a Roman eagle, at the end of the street. Towards the close of day, this sunlight turned rose-red as if mixed with blood, and it gave its colour to everything that stood in its path as it filtered along the narrow street. It painted the potter's pots and the plank squealing under the carpenter's saw, and it coloured, too, the white wimple that surrounded Mary's face.

But loveliest of all was the way the sunshine gleamed from the small puddles that had gathered between the big, uneven stones that paved the street. Quite suddenly Jesus poked his hand down into the puddle nearest him. It had occurred to him that he should paint his grey birds with the sparkling sunshine that gave the water and the walls of the houses and everything around him such a beautiful colour.

The sunshine was pleased to let itself be captured like

the colours on an artist's palette, and when Jesus painted it on his little clay birds, it stayed there, cloaking them with a diamond-like brilliance from head to foot.

Every now and then Judas would cast a glance over at Jesus to see whether he was making more and prettier birds than he was. And when he saw how Jesus was painting his clay birds with the sunshine taken from the puddles in the street, he gave a cry of delight. And now Judas, too, dipped his hand in the bright water and tried to capture the sunshine.

But the sunshine refused to be captured by him. It slipped out between his fingers, sliding away however quickly he tried to move his hands, and he was unable to catch even a pinch of colour for his poor birds.

'Wait now, Judas,' Jesus said. 'I shall come and paint your birds.'

'No,' Judas replied. 'You mustn't touch them. They are good enough just as they are.'

He stood up with furrowed brow and lips pursed. Then he placed his big foot on his birds and, one by one, flattened them into little lumps of clay.

When all his birds were destroyed, he walked over to Jesus, who was stroking his small clay birds, which glistened like jewels. Judas looked at them in silence, but then he raised his foot and stamped on one of them.

When Judas took his foot away and saw the small bird reduced to grey clay, he felt such a sense of relief that he began to laugh as he raised his foot to trample on another one.

'Judas!' Jesus shouted, 'what are you doing? Don't you know that they are alive and can sing?'

But Judas just laughed and stamped on another bird.

Jesus looked around for help. Judas was big and Jesus was not strong enough to stop him. He looked around for his mother. She was not far away, but before she could reach them, Judas would have time to destroy all the birds. Jesus's eyes filled with tears. Judas had already trampled on four of his birds and there were only three remaining.

Jesus was vexed at his birds for just staying there, not heeding the danger and allowing themselves to be trampled. He clapped his hands to wake them, and he called to them: 'Fly, fly!'

The three birds began to move their little wings and, flapping anxiously, they managed to fly up to the edge of the roof where they would be safe.

When Judas saw the birds take wing at Jesus's words, he began to weep. He tore his hair as he had seen old people do when they were in great anxiety and sorrow, and he threw himself down at Jesus's feet.

Judas lay there, rolling like a dog in the dirt before Jesus, kissing his feet and bidding him to raise his foot and stamp on him as he had done to the clay birds.

For Judas loved Jesus, admired him and idolized him at the same time as hating him.

Mary, who had been watching the children play the whole time, now rose, picked Judas up, sat him on her lap and stroked him.

'You poor child,' she said to him. 'You don't know that

you have attempted something that no one in the world is capable of. Do not try anything like that again unless you want to become the unhappiest of men! How could things possibly turn out for anyone who tries to compete with him who paints with the rays of sunshine and breathes the spirit of life into dead clay?'

Redbreast

It was in the time when Our Lord created the world, when He created not only Heaven and Earth but also all the creatures and plants and gave them their names, as well.

Many stories are told of that time, and anyone who knew each and every one of them would also hold the key to all those things in the world that we currently cannot understand.

One day during that time, Our Lord happened to be in Paradise painting the birds, and the paint in His paint pots ran out. The goldfinch would have been left colourless if Our Lord had not cleaned all His brushes on her plumage.

And it was then that the donkey got her long ears because she could not remember what name she had been given. She forgot it as soon as she took a few steps in the meadows of Paradise, and three times she had to come back and ask what she was called, until Our Lord grew a little impatient with her, took her by both ears and said: 'Your name is donkey, donkey, donkey.'

As He spoke, He pulled on her ears to improve her sense of hearing, so that she would remember what she was told.

And it was on the very same day that the bee was given

its punishment. For as soon as the bee was made, she immediately started collecting nectar, and animals and humans who caught the delightful scent of the honey were drawn to it and wanted to taste it. But the bee wanted to keep it all to herself and used her poisonous stings to chase away all those who came near the honeycomb. Our Lord saw this and at once He called the bee to Him and punished her.

'I gave you the gift of gathering nectar for honey, the loveliest food in Creation,' said Our Lord, 'but I did not thereby give you the right to treat your neighbour harshly. Now know this: every time you sting someone who wants your honey, you must die!'

And yes, it was then that the cricket went blind and the ant lost its wings; so many extraordinary things happened that day.

Our Lord, great and gentle, sat there all day long creating and conjuring, and towards evening He had the notion of making a little grey bird.

'Remember that your name is Redbreast!' Our Lord said to the bird, once He was finished. And He set him in His open hand and let him fly.

When the bird had flown around for a while and gazed upon the beautiful Earth where he was to live, he felt the urge to look at himself. Then he saw that he was entirely grey and his breast was as grey as all the rest. Redbreast turned this way and that, looking at his reflection in the water, but he could not detect a single red feather.

So the bird flew back to Our Lord.

Our Lord, good and gentle, sat there letting His hands generate butterflies, which fluttered around His head. He had doves cooing on His shoulders, and from the ground around Him, the rose, the lily and the daisy grew up into the light.

The little bird's heart pounded with apprehension, but he advanced closer and closer to Our Lord in airy arcs until he finally alighted on His hand.

Then Our Lord asked him what he wanted.

'There is something I would like to ask you about,' said the little bird.

'What do you want to know?' said Our Lord.

'Why should my name be Redbreast, when I am entirely grey from my beak to the very tip of my tail? Why am I called Redbreast when I do not possess a single red feather?'

The bird looked imploringly at Our Lord with his little black eyes and turned his head. All around him he saw pheasants, red all over beneath a dusting of gold, parrots with luxuriant red neck ruffs, cockerels with red combs, not to mention butterflies, goldfish and roses. Naturally, he thought about how little it would take, just a single little drop on his breast, to help him live up to his name.

'Why should I be called Redbreast when I am all grey?' the bird asked again, waiting for Our Lord to say: 'Ah my friend, I see that I have forgotten to paint your breast feathers red, yet wait a moment, and it shall be done.'

But Our Lord merely gave a serene smile and said, 'I named you Redbreast and Redbreast you shall be called, but it is up to you to see if you can earn your red breast feathers.'

With that, Our Lord raised His hand and sent the bird flying out into the world once more.

The bird flew down to Paradise, deep in thought. What could a little bird like him do to get himself some red feathers?

The only thing he could think of was to take up residence in a thorn bush. He built his nest in among the spikes of a dense thicket of thorns. It was as if he was expecting a rose petal to plaster itself to his throat and lend him its colour.

An immense number of years had passed after this day that was the most joyous day on Earth. Since that time, both animals and humans had left Paradise and spread out across the world. And the human beings had made such strides that they had now learned to cultivate the land and traverse the oceans, they had devised clothes and ornaments and yes, they had long since learned to build great temples and mighty towns such as Thebes, Rome and Jerusalem.

Then a new day dawned which would also long be remembered in the history of the world. On that day, the bird who went by the name of Redbreast was perched on a small bare hill outside the walls of Jerusalem, singing for his babies, who were resting in a little nest in a low thorn bush.

Redbreast told his little ones about the wonders of

Creation Day and the giving of names, the same story that every bird called Redbreast had told, including the very first one who had heard God's words and been released from God's hand.

'And now, you see,' he said ruefully, 'so many years have gone by, so many roses have come into bud, so many chicks have hatched from their eggs since Creation Day that no one can count them, but Redbreast is still a little grey bird. He has not yet found a way of earning his red breast feathers.'

The chicks stretched their mouths wide and asked if their forefathers had tried to accomplish any great deeds to earn the priceless red colour.

'We all did what we could,' said the little bird, 'but we all failed. The very first Redbreast once met another bird who was just like him and instantly experienced such fierce love for this bird that he felt his breast glowing. Ah, he thought, now I understand. It is Our Lord's intention for me to love so ardently that my breast feathers will be turned red by the fiery love that resides in my heart. But he failed, just as all who came after him failed, and as you, too, will fail.'

The baby birds chirped in distress. They were already lamenting the fact that the colour red would never decorate their downy little breasts.

'We also had high hopes of our song,' said the adult bird, speaking in slow and disconsolate tones. 'The very first Redbreast started it, his song making his breast swell with rapture, and he dared to hope again. Ah, he thought, it is the passionate singing, rooted in my soul, that will turn my breast feathers red. But he failed, just as all who came after him failed, and as you, too, will fail.'

Once again there was a sorrowful cheeping from the chicks' still semi-naked throats.

'We also placed our hope in our pluckiness and bravery. The very first Redbreast fought bravely with other birds and his breast was aflame with pugnacious spirit. Ah, he thought, my breast feathers will be turned red by the urge to fight which glows within my heart. But he failed, just as all who came after him failed, and as you, too, will fail.'

The baby birds cheeped boldly that they nevertheless wanted to try to earn the coveted privilege, but the bird replied sadly that it would be impossible. What could they hope for, when so many excellent forefathers had not succeeded in reaching their goal? What more could they do but love, sing and fight? What could . . .

The bird stopped in mid-sentence, for a crowd of people came flooding out of the gates of Jerusalem, and the whole throng advanced up the hill where the bird had its nest.

There were knights on proud horses, soldiers with long spears, executioners' men with hammers and nails, priests and judges in dignified procession, weeping women and above all a wild and motley crowd – an unpleasant, howling band of street loiterers.

The little grey bird perched on the edge of his nest, all of a quiver. He feared that the little thorn bush would be trampled underfoot at any moment and his babies would perish.

'Preserve yourselves,' he cried to the defenceless little chicks. 'Huddle together and stay quiet! Here comes a horse, about to tread on us! Here comes a soldier with iron-shod sandals! Here comes the whole wild multitude, rushing towards us!'

The little bird abruptly ceased his warning cries and went quiet and still. He almost forgot the looming danger.

All at once he jumped down into the nest and extended his wings over his nestlings.

'No, this is too awful,' he said. 'I do not want you to see this sight. Three wrongdoers are going to be crucified.'

And he spread out his wings so that the chicks could not see anything. They were aware only of resounding hammer blows, wails of distress and the unruly hoots of the crowd.

Redbreast followed the whole spectacle, his eyes widening in horror. He could not take his eyes off the three wretched figures.

'How cruel humans are!' said the bird a short while later. 'It is not enough for them to nail these poor creatures to the cross, but they have even fixed a crown of sharp thorns onto the head of one of them.'

'I can see that the thorns have lacerated his forehead and made the blood flow,' he went on. 'And this is such a fine man, looking around with such a gentle gaze that every single person ought to love him. It pierces my heart like the point of an arrow to see him suffer.'

The little bird felt a swelling sense of compassion for the man crowned with thorns.

'If I were my brother the eagle,' he thought, 'I would pull the nails out of his hands and use my strong talons to drive away all those who torment him.'

He saw blood trickling down the forehead of the crucified man and could no longer sit still in his nest.

'I may be small and weak, but I should still be able to do something for this poor sufferer in his torment,' thought the bird. And he left the nest and took to the air, swooping in wide circles around the crucified man.

He circled him several times before daring to approach, for he was a shy little bird who had never risked getting too close to a human. But he eventually summoned up the courage, flew over and used his beak to pull out a thorn that had pierced the brow of the man on the cross.

As he did so, a drop of the crucified man's blood fell onto the bird's breast. It swiftly pooled and spread, colouring all the delicate little feathers of the breast.

The crucified man parted his lips and whispered to the bird. 'For your mercy's sake you have gained what your species has been trying to attain ever since the world was created.'

As soon as the bird returned to the nest, his young cried out to him, 'Your breast is red! Your breast feathers are redder than roses!'

'It is only a drop of blood from that poor man's forehead,' said the bird. 'It will go as soon as I bathe in a brook or a clear spring.'

But no matter how many baths the little bird took, the red colour did not leave his breast, and when his chicks were full grown, the blood-red patch shone brightly on their breast feathers, too, as it does on the throat and breast of every Redbreast to this very day.

The Skull

There once was a man in the parish of Svartsjö in Värmland who went from door to door one Christmas Eve, inviting everyone in the district to come to his home for dinner, but could find no one willing to leave their own home that day. He ranged far and wide, but finally, as it was starting to get dark and he had not been able to tempt a single guest to join him, he realized he had no choice but to return home with nothing to show for his excursion.

The man should have told himself that no other outcome was to be expected and taken the matter with equanimity, yet he did not, and instead remained extremely vexed by all those refusals. He had laid on supplies of food and schnapps at home and his wife was busy preparing for a feast. Where was the pleasure in that, though, when not one cheery comrade would keep him company at the Christmas dinner table? 'It must be that they all think too highly of themselves to accept my hospitality,' he told himself. 'It is because I have become a gravedigger that they do not consider it grand enough to celebrate Christmas Eve in my home.'

This accusation was entirely unfair, because, say what you like about the folk of Svartsjö, it would never have occurred to any of them to turn down an invitation on the grounds that it came from someone too lowly. Nor was this man merely a simple gravedigger. His name was Anders Öster and he came from a long line of fiddlers. He himself had been an army musician in the Värmland Regiment and it was only after receiving an honourable discharge from active service that he had taken on the job of gravedigger.

What was more, he was not only the gravedigger but also the verger, a post that has nothing off-putting about it, but in his current frame of mind he dwelt only on the darker side of life.

'As no one wants to come and join me, I suppose I will have to invite some ghosts from the churchyard,' he muttered. 'At least they will not be ashamed to attend a party at the gravedigger's place.'

He was just passing the old granite wall that encloses Svartsjö churchyard and naturally that was what put such a thought into his head, although for the time being he had no intention of putting it into practice.

But when he had taken a few steps more, he caught sight of a round, white object poking out of the dry grass at the edge of the footpath. It had a much whiter gleam to it than any ordinary stone and he stopped to see what manner of thing it could be. Peering through the pale twilight, he was able to make out that it was nothing less than a skull. It had most likely been thrown up along with gravel and earth when he was digging a grave the previous day and dragged to its present position by some animal.

In normal circumstances, the man would undoubtedly

have picked up this human relic, which could have been one of his forebears who, if nothing else, had lived and died in his own home parish, and carried it into the mortuary, but he was not inclined to do anything so simple and natural. Instead, he raised his hat, bowed to the skull with a smile and addressed it in the strangely mild and melodious voice that he rarely used except when he was in his most dangerous mood.

'Good evening, good evening,' he said, 'and well met! Let me firstly wish you a Merry Christmas, and secondly tell you that I'm going around giving out party invitations. I wonder whether you consider yourself above coming to join me this evening. It is not a grand gathering, you understand, but you shall have as much food and schnapps as you like.'

With his invitation delivered he stood there, hat in hand, as if awaiting a reply.

'Well, you aren't saying no, at any rate,' he went on, once he had waited for a reasonable length of time, 'so I suppose I can hope that you will come. I live over there in that big building in front of the church, so you won't have far to go for the party.'

Then Anders Öster let out a loud, wild laugh, put his hat on his head and went home without any further stops along the way.

Indeed, he was the churchyard's nearest neighbour, as he lived in the parish meeting hall, where he had a couple of small rooms in the attic. He crossed the porch and opened the door, and the sight that met his eyes was certainly not designed to improve his mood. His wife was on her knees just inside the door, scrubbing the entrance hall. There was a thin little tallow candle in a copper candlestick on the wet floor in front of her, casting light on her scouring brush, water tub and floorcloths.

'Well, it's a fine thing for you still to be at your scrubbing when guests could arrive any minute,' said the man as he stepped inside.

She looked up, her face surprisingly attractive with its clear, noble features, and cast a quick glance in his direction. She saw at once how things stood.

'So nobody wanted to come, then?' she said. 'It is as I expected. Who has ever heard of folk accepting other people's invitations for Christmas Eve?'

'No, they were all too comfortable where they were,' he said, with a vehemence that made it sound like an accusation hurled in her direction. 'But I did get one acceptance, as it happens,' he said nonchalantly, 'although he won't be coming until a bit later.'

'Go up to our rooms and wait for him!' said his wife. 'There is light and I have set the table. I shall be finished here very shortly.'

But Anders Öster was not remotely inclined to do as he was bidden. He stood his ground in the hallway, blocking his wife from her housework. He knew full well what he was doing and it gave him a bitter sense of satisfaction.

To his right, the door was open to the parish meeting room, a large space where the local parishioners would hold their councils and meetings. A hearty fire blazed in the open hearth, illuminating the whole room, and Anders Öster stood there, looking in. The room was old-fashioned in style, with walls of plain, rough-hewn timber, huge floorboards and exposed roof beams. Solid benches attached to the walls ran all the way round the room, a large, unpainted wooden table with turned legs stood right in one corner, diagonally across from the door, and at the table there was a chairman's seat, high-backed, leather-upholstered, a true symbol of dependable authority and imperturbable order.

His wife had scrubbed the floor in there, too, and strewn it with white sand and chopped juniper twigs. In the dancing glow of the blazing fire the room seemed substantial and agreeable to Anders Öster and he said to his wife:

'When you've finished, you can bring down the Christmas food and set it out here in the parish meeting room. I think I would like to hold my Christmas feast here.'

His wife looked up in dismay.

'Whatever do you mean?' she said. 'Are you going to sit down here and drink with that guest you are expecting? There is nothing to cover the windows. If anyone were to walk by, then the two of you would be in full view.'

She was greatly agitated. The meeting room, like the church, belonged to the parish, and for her it was an almost sacred space. She could not conceive of it being put to use for a drinking bout.

But Anders Öster was not prepared to be thwarted in his every wish that day.

'Don't argue, Bolla!' he said. 'I tell you I want to have my Christmas dinner in here this evening!'

It was the great table, the great chair and the great room that attracted him. If he could have his Christmas feast seated in such a venerable chair, eating his meal at a table that could easily accommodate another twenty or thirty guests, where all the powerful figures of the community were wont to gather, he would feel like a respected man, a well-to-do farmer, and that was what he needed.

'You will most certainly lose your job, if you do that,' said his wife. 'For as long as I live, you will not be tempted into this madness.'

When he heard his wife take against his wishes with such determination, his fury knew no bounds. All the despondency that had accumulated inside him in the course of the day came boiling up to the surface in search of an outlet. He did not say a word in reply but ran upstairs to the attic and into their rooms, where he took his shotgun down from the wall.

Then he crept lightly back across the attic to the stairs and leaned over the banisters so he could see his wife, who was still on her knees scrubbing the floor of the entrance hall.

'Bolla, Bolla,' he said in a voice so soft and silky that it was virtually dripping with honey, 'is it your opinion that I shall not eat my Christmas dinner at the table of the parish meeting room for as long as you are still alive?'

'Yes it is,' she called back readily, but as she said the words it struck her that nothing good ever came of that melodious tone of voice. She looked upwards and saw the shiny muzzle of a gun a few yards above her head.

She threw herself backwards. At that instant the hall was filled with smoke and fire and a bullet struck the floor right in front of her.

'Lord Almighty!' She abandoned her brush and tub and fled headlong into the night.

Anders Öster made no attempt to follow her. He gave a cold, shrill laugh, just as he had done on the path a short time before. Then he went calmly back upstairs with his shotgun and hung it in its place.

After that he swiftly and deftly set about arranging everything the way he wanted it. He pushed the cleaning things into a corner of the front hall so he had clear passage and then brought everything his wife had laid out for the feast down to the parish meeting room. He laid a cloth on the council table, set out two decorative branched candles, and between them a dish with a big pat of butter, elaborately curled and decorated; then he brought down several kinds of bread, cheeses both rich and of the simpler kind, sausage and ham, a leg of mutton, a jug of Christmas ale and some knives and plates. Last of all he struggled downstairs with the cask of schnapps, which he put in the middle of the table with a ring of glasses below the tap.

When everything was in order, he sat down in the chairman's seat and ate and drank with a huge sense of well-being.

Probably all the anger that had built up inside him, to

the point where every limb ached, had been discharged with the shot he had fired. He felt so relieved that he could only think he had done the right thing.

Why should his wife stand up to him in this innocent wish of his? After all, it was her duty to obey her husband. Now she had got what she deserved. It was proper justice that he had meted out to her by his actions, and it was not only just, it was also wise.

He sat there reminding himself of numerous other occasions when she had been obstinate. But now there would be an end to all of that. Now he had taught her who was the master of the house. It had been a really inspired idea to let off that shot at her; from now on he would be able to enjoy better days and derive greater comfort from his marriage.

He was both tired and hungry and tucked into the spread with gusto. After a while, beginning to feel full, he once again started to regret that he had not been able to enlist any company.

All at once he remembered the skull. 'I do believe he intends to do the same as everyone else and not bother to come,' he said. 'Maybe there will be nothing for it but for me to go out and fetch him.'

He put on his hat, went the few steps to the churchyard and was soon on his way back with the skull in his hand.

It had a good amount of soil stuck to it and he dipped it in the tub of scrubbing water and wiped it dry with one of the floorcloths. When he had made it as presentable as he could, he stood it on the table in front of him.

His wife, meanwhile, shaken and with eyes red from weeping, was at a farmhouse just a few steps from the church. She had been taken in by good friends and neighbours, who tried to console her, and as it was Christmas Eve she did her very best to at least stop crying, so she would not ruin their festive enjoyment with her moans of despair. But she felt as if she was staring down into an abyss that she would now have to plunge into. 'He shot at me,' she thought, over and over. 'He tried to kill me. What is to become of us?'

If he had been drunk, she would have paid it no heed. But he was sober, and he had tried to kill her over a trifling matter.

She thought back over the long time they had lived with one another. They had stuck together through thick and thin for over twenty years and now it had come to this: he had shot at her; there was not the least trace of affection for her in his heart after all the hardship and all the troubles they had been through together.

At the farm where she had taken refuge there were a couple of small boys, who were extraordinarily interested in the entire proceedings. They kept on running out to peer through the windows of the parish meeting room and came back to tell her what they had seen. 'Now he's bringing food downstairs and laying it out on the big parish council table,' they reported. A while later it was: 'Now he's in the chairman's seat, eating and drinking.'

The next time they told her that he was still in his seat and now talking, for all the world as if he had someone in the room with him. He raised his glass in a toast to someone the children could not see.

His wife showed little curiosity in what her husband was doing. She could think only of one thing: the fact that he had shot at her. To think that the man who had promised to love her for better or worse had shot at her!

She felt it would be impossible to go back to him. It was not so much the thought that she would have to live in permanent terror of a husband who took up his gun at the slightest opposition that stopped her returning to his house. It was rather the heart-stopping sensation that he must hate her, as he was capable of attacking her in such a way.

It was an irreparable rift. It could not be remedied, could not be undone. The very foundation on which they had built their happiness was shattered. There was no longer any solid base for it.

Repeated shudders ran through her as she helped the farmer's wife to stir the rice porridge and lay the Christmas table. 'His shot killed me anyway,' she thought. 'It went straight through my heart.'

She had just taken her seat at the festive table with the others when the door slowly opened and her husband came in. He did not step forward into the room but stayed in the shadows over by the door. He did not gesture to her to come to him, did not move a muscle, simply stood there.

In those first moments she felt nothing but indignation at his daring to come near her and she forced herself not to look at him or show any awareness of his presence. But naturally she could not help sending a glance or two towards the door and she was surprised to see him standing so still. 'Something's happened to him,' she thought. 'He isn't the same as he was before. He's all white in the face. He must have been taken ill. Maybe he was running a fever when he shot at me just now.'

She got up from the table and said quietly, 'Thank you for having me,' and crossed the room to the door. The man opened it and went ahead of her out of the house and over to the parish meeting room. He walked in silence the whole way and she felt as if she was following his ghost rather than the man himself.

She knew, of course, that he had set out the feast in the parish meeting room, but there was no sign of it now and everything had been set back in order. He went upstairs to their own rooms in the attic. There, too, everything looked as it had when she had fled from home.

The only object that was unfamiliar to her was a skull standing on a table in the corner of the room. The man went over to the table and pointed at the skull.

'Look at it!' he said.

She did so, but did not notice anything strange about it.

'Can you see that he has been shot – murdered even?' he said. 'He did not kill himself. The shot came from behind, just behind the ear, here.'

'Yes, I can see that,' she said, feeling herself gradually suffused with a quaking sense of expectation.

'Can you remember ever hearing about anybody being

shot in this parish? No, nothing like that has happened in our time, or in our parents' time, either. It is very rare for anyone to be murdered in these parts, very rare. This could be the only body buried in the churchyard soil whose skull has been holed by a murderer's bullet, and now here it is in front of me.'

His wife held still.

'It was lying in my path as I came home this evening. It clearly wanted to show itself to me, but I didn't look at it very closely at the time. Later, as I sat here alone, it kept coming into my mind, so in the end I was obliged to go and fetch it. I thought it would be a pity for it to lie out in the cold and darkness and, besides, I wanted somebody to talk to. And when I put it down on the table in front of me and poured a glass so I could raise a toast to it, I saw that it had been blasted by a shot. What do you say to that, Bolla? Where has he come from, and why did he come to be in my way on this of all evenings? How was it that I had to bring it in here, just after I had shot at you?'

'It must have been God,' she whispered, putting her hands together.

'Yes,' he replied, and he too was whispering. 'That must be it. This was God's will. He particularly wanted me to see this. It was meant to show me what I had tried to do. It was sent to me so I would understand my great sin and wretchedness.'

They moved closer together. They found themselves automatically taking each other's hand and they stood before the skull. It was indeed sent to them by God. By its presence it told them that God was looking after them, that He had compassion for them and wanted to save them.

All at once they felt that everything else was of no importance. The wife did not demand that her husband tell her he regretted what he had done. She had completely forgotten that she no longer wanted to live with him. The husband had no further thoughts about which of them would rule over the house. They could have been a thousand times more vexed with each other, they could have had a thousand times as many reasons to reproach each other, and it would all have been forgotten in the face of the blissful certainty that God had them in His care and wanted to save them from coming to hate one another.

God wished them well, and that was why He had sent a messenger bearing a warning. Faced with something of such magnificence they forgot not only their anger with each other but also their poverty and their anxieties about the future. They felt the greatest joy that mortals can experience.

The Animals' New Year's Night

One New Year's night several hundred years ago, the rural dean of Delsbo was riding through a dense forest. Mounted on his horse, he was dressed in his fur coat and hat, and on the pommel of his saddle he had a bag which held the communion cup and plate, his prayer book and his clerical gown. He had been called to make a parish visit deep in the forest district and had stayed talking to the sick man until late at night. Now he was on his way home at last and not expecting to reach it until long after midnight.

Since he was out on horseback rather than comfortably at home in bed, he was pleased that it was not a bad night. The weather was calm and mild, despite the overcast sky. A big, round full moon was hidden behind the clouds but still gave some light even though it could not itself be seen. Had it not been for that small amount of moonlight he would have found it hard to pick out the path, there being no snow on the ground and everything looking the same brownish-grey colour.

That night, the dean was riding a horse that he had great respect for: a strong beast with plenty of staying power, almost as clever as a human being. Among its many virtues was its ability to find its way home from anywhere in the parish. The dean had noticed this on many occasions and he had so much confidence in it that he never bothered to think about his route when he was riding that particular horse. Which was why he was now riding through the wilds of the forest in the dark of night with the reins hanging loose and his thoughts far away.

The dean was thinking about many things, not least the sermon he was going to deliver the next day, and so it was quite a long time before it occurred to him to check how far he still had to go to get home. When he did at last look up, he was surprised to see that the forest surrounding him was still as dense as at the start of his journey. He had been riding for so long that he really ought to have come to the farming area of his parish by now.

In those days, the parish of Delsbo was just the same as it is now. The church, the deanery and all the big farms lay in the northern part of it around the Dellen lakes, whereas the south consisted of nothing but forest and hills. When the dean realized he was still out in the wilderness he knew that he must be in the southern part of his parish and that he needed to ride north in order to get home. But he felt sure that he was not doing so. He had neither the moon nor the stars to guide him, but he was one of those people who have the points of the compass in their heads and he now had a distinct feeling that he was riding south or perhaps east.

His first thought was to turn his horse round, but then he stopped himself. This horse had never taken the wrong road before so it was unlikely to be doing so now; it was much more likely that he was the one who was mistaken.

He had been so preoccupied that he had not been paying attention to the route, so he let the horse continue in the same direction as before and sank back into his thoughts.

No sooner had he done so than a large branch struck him so hard that it very nearly swept him out of the saddle, making him realize that he really did need to pay attention to where he was.

He looked down at the ground and saw that he was riding on soft moss with no path in sight. But the horse was moving along quite briskly nonetheless and showed no signs of hesitation. Nevertheless, just as before, the dean was convinced he was going in the wrong direction.

This time he did not hesitate. He took firm hold of the reins, forced the horse to turn and succeeded in getting it back on the main path, but no sooner was it there than it turned aside once more and set off straight into the forest again.

The dean was utterly convinced that the animal was going in the wrong direction, but since the horse was being so stubborn, he assumed the beast was trying to find a better route and he let it continue.

The horse was managing well even though there was no path for it to follow. When it came to a steep slope, it climbed it as nimbly as a goat, and when going downhill, it put its feet together and slid down the steep, slabby rocks.

'I just hope he finds the way home before morning service!' the dean thought. 'I can just imagine the look on the Delsbo parishioners' faces if I don't make it to church on time.'

He did not have to ponder that thought for long as they soon arrived at a place he recognized. It was a small dark tarn which he had visited for fishing the summer before. He realized now that things were just as he had feared: he was in the very depths of the forest and the horse had been heading south-east, as if it was really intending to carry him as far from his church and home as possible.

The dean leapt from the saddle. He simply could not allow the horse to take him off into wild and uninhabited areas. He had to get home, and if the horse was going to stubbornly insist on going in the wrong direction, he decided he would go on foot and lead the horse until they were back on familiar paths. He wound the reins around his arm and began walking. Travelling through the forest dressed in a heavy fur coat was not exactly easy, but the dean was a strong and tough man who was not afraid of hard work.

The horse immediately began to cause more problems. It did not want to follow him, dug its hooves into the ground and resisted.

Now the dean lost his temper. He was not in the habit of striking that particular horse and he had no desire to start doing so now. Instead, he simply dropped the reins and stepped away from it. 'This is where we part,' he said, 'since you want to go your own way.'

He had walked no more than a few paces before the horse caught up with him, carefully took hold of his sleeve and tried to hold him back. The dean turned round and looked into the horse's eyes as if trying to work out why it was behaving so strangely.

Afterwards the dean could never really understand how it could have been possible, but the fact is that, dark as it was, he could see the horse's face clearly and he could read it just as if it was the face of a human being. He recognized then that the horse was in the most fearful state of anxiety and that it was gazing at him with a look that was both imploring and reproachful. 'Day after day I have served you and done your will,' it seemed to be saying. 'Can't you follow me for just this one night?'

The dean was touched by the prayer he read in the animal's eyes. It was clear that in one way or other the horse needed his help that night and, being one man in a thousand, he decided he would follow his horse. Without any further delay, he led the horse over to a rock which he then used to climb into the saddle.

'On you go now!' he said. 'Since you want me to be with you, I shan't desert you. No one will be able to say that the dean of Delsbo refused to accompany a creature in need.'

After this he concentrated on staying in the saddle and allowed the horse to go where it wanted. Their journey was a dangerous and difficult one and led uphill almost the whole way. The forest closed in so tight around them that the dean could not see two steps in front, but he sensed they were making their way up a high mountain. The horse worked its way up terrifying slopes and if the dean himself had been in charge it would never have occurred to him to take a horse into such terrain.

'You're surely not thinking of climbing up Blacksåsen,

are you?' the dean said with a little laugh, because he knew that Blacksåsen was one of the highest mountains in Hälsingland.

As the journey progressed the dean became aware that he and the horse were not the only ones on the move that night. He could hear stones rattling and the crack of branches breaking. It sounded as though large animals were pushing their way through the forest. He knew that there were many wolves in the district and he wondered if the horse was leading him into a battle with wild beasts.

Upwards, ever upwards they went, and the higher they climbed, the sparser the forest became.

Eventually they rode out onto an almost bare mountainside and the dean was able to look round in all directions. He looked out over an enormous sweep of country that rose and fell in hummocks and hills, all of which were cloaked in dark forests. It was so dark that he found it hard to make sense of anything, but he soon worked out where he was.

'Well, well, it can only be Blacksåsen that I have ridden up,' he thought. 'It can't be any other mountain. Over there to the west I can see the rocky outcrops at Järvsö and, over there to the east, that must be the Baltic Sea around the island of Agön. I can see something else glinting up in the north – that must be the Dellen lakes. And down here right below me I can see the white foam of the Nämforsen Rapids. Yes, it's Blacksåsen I've climbed, all right. What an adventure!'

Once they had reached the very top of the mountain,

the horse halted behind a bushy spruce tree as if wanting to stay out of sight. The dean leaned forward and bent some branches aside so that he had a clear view.

The bare crown of the mountain lay before him, but it was far from empty and desolate as he had expected it to be. In the middle of the open ground stood a huge boulder and all around it was a large gathering of wild beasts that looked, the dean thought, as if they had come there to hold some sort of assembly.

The dean saw that closest to the big rock were the bears, and they were so heavily and solidly built that they looked like fur-covered boulders themselves. They were lying down, their small eyes blinking impatiently. It was obvious they had risen from hibernation to attend the gathering and were finding it difficult to stay awake. Behind them there were several hundred wolves sitting in close ranks. There was nothing sleepy about them, they were more alive in the darkness of winter than they ever were in summer. They were sitting on their hindquarters like dogs, lashing the ground with their tails and panting heavily with their tongues hanging out of their gaping mouths. Behind the wolves there were lynx creeping around, clumsy and stiff-legged like great deformed cats. They seemed to shrink from showing themselves in front of the other animals and they spat if anyone came too close to them. The row behind them was occupied by the wolverines with their dog-like faces and their bear-like fur. They did not like being down on the ground and were stamping their broad feet impatiently, longing to be back up in the trees. And behind them, covering the whole of the space back to the edge of the trees, jostled foxes, weasels and martens, all of them small and beautifully formed, but all looking even wilder and more bloodthirsty than the larger animals.

All this was visible to the dean because the whole area was brightly lit; standing there, on the large rock in the middle of the gathering, was a forest witch holding a torch of blazing pine wood that burned with a high red flame. The witch was as tall as the tallest tree in the forest; she was clad in a cloak of spruce brushwood and her hair was formed of spruce cones. She was standing absolutely still, her face turned towards the forest, spying and listening intently.

Although the dean could see it all quite clearly, he was so amazed that he struggled against it, not wanting to believe the evidence of his own eyes. 'This is quite impossible, quite impossible,' he thought. 'I have spent too long riding around in the darkness of the forest. My imagination has got the better of me.'

But he paid close attention to everything anyway, wondering what was going to happen and what he was going to see.

He did not have long to wait before he heard the tinkling of a little bell down in the forest. Immediately after that, he heard the noise of feet and the crashing of branches as when a host of animals is breaking a path through wild country.

A great herd of farm animals was making its way up

the mountain. They came out of the forest in the same order as when they went to the summer pastures. At the front walked the lead cow wearing her bell, then came the bull, then the other cows, followed by the younger animals and calves. Behind them came the sheep in a tight flock, then the goats, and lastly a couple of horses and foals. The farm dog was walking alongside the herd, but there was neither a herd boy nor girl accompanying it.

The dean found it heart-rending to see all these farm animals advancing straight towards their predators. He would have liked to step out in front of them and shout at them to stop, but he realized that it was not within the power of any human being to halt the animals' progress on such a night and so he remained silent.

The farm animals were obviously troubled by what they had to face, and their sadness and anxiety showed. Even the bell-cow walked with despairing steps, her head hanging low. The goats had no desire to play or to butt one another. The horses tried to put a brave face on it but their bodies were trembling with terror. Most pitiful of all was the dog, which was almost crawling along the ground with its tail between its legs.

The bell-cow led the procession right up to the forest witch who was standing there on the rock on the summit of the mountain. The cow walked around the rock and then turned back towards the forest without any of the wild animals touching it. And all the rest of the livestock also passed the wild beasts unharmed.

But as the beasts filed past, the dean noticed how the

witch lowered her blazing torch over some of them so that it pointed downwards. Each time this happened a loud roar of rejoicing rang out among the predators, particularly when the torch was lowered over a cow or one of the larger animals, but the animal picked out by the torch in this way would utter a shrill scream as if a knife had been sunk into its flesh, and the whole flock to which that animal belonged would begin lamenting.

Now the dean began to understand what he was seeing. He had heard before how all the animals in the parish of Delsbo gathered up on Blacksåsen during New Year's Night for the forest witch to pick out those that would fall victim to predators during the coming year. He felt great pity for these poor beasts, subject as they were to the power of their wild enemies when mankind should have been their only masters.

The first herd had scarcely passed before the sound of a bell could be heard from the forest once again and the livestock from another farm made their way up to the top of the mountain. The beasts walked forward in the same order as the previous herd and the forest witch, stern and unyielding, marked out animal after animal for death. And after this herd there came another, and then another, endlessly. Some of them were so small that they consisted of no more than a single cow and a few sheep, others were just a few goats, and although it was obvious that these came from poor and needy households, they were still forced to pass before the forest witch and still no mercy was shown.

The dean thought of the farmers of Delsbo and of the great love they had for their animals. 'If they knew about this, they would never allow it to happen,' he thought. 'They would risk their own lives rather than allow their livestock to be paraded before wolves and bears and sentenced by the forest witch.'

The very last herd to come forward was the dean's own herd. The dean recognized the sound of his lead cow's bell in the distance, and his horse must have known it, too, for it began to shudder all over and was bathed in sweat.

'I see,' the dean said to his horse, 'so now it's your turn to pass the forest witch and receive your sentence. But do not fear! Now I understand why you brought me here and I will not desert you.'

All the fine animals from the dean's farm emerged in a long line from the forest and approached the forest witch and the wild predators. Last in line walked the horse that had carried its master to the summit of Blacksåsen. The dean remained in the saddle and let the horse carry him towards the forest witch.

He had neither gun nor knife to defend himself, but he had taken out his Prayer Book and sat with it pressed against his breast as he went into battle against evil.

At first it seemed as if none of those present noticed him. The livestock from his home farm paraded past the forest witch in the same manner as all the other herds, but the witch did not lower her torch over any of them. Only when the wise horse stepped forward did the forest witch prepare to mark it with the sign of death. But at that very moment the dean held up the Prayer Book and the light of the blazing torch fell on the cross on its cover. The forest witch uttered a shrill scream and the torch fell from her hand to the ground.

The flame died immediately and in the sudden transition from light to darkness the dean could see nothing. Nor could he hear any sound. All around him was nothing but the deep silence that usually reigns in the wilderness in winter.

Then the heavy clouds that covered the heavens suddenly parted and through the gap the full moon cast its light down upon the earth beneath. And the dean saw that now he and his horse were standing alone on the summit of Blacksåsen and not a single one of the wild beasts remained. Nor was the ground trampled and churned by the many herds that had passed. But the dean himself was still holding his Prayer Book out in front of him and his horse was still trembling and bathed in sweat.

After he had ridden down the mountain and returned home to his farm, the dean was no longer sure whether what he had witnessed had been a dream, a vision or reality. One thing he did know: that this was an exhortation to him to remember the poor animals that lived under the threat of the wild beasts. He preached this to the farmers of Delsbo so powerfully that, in his time, all the bears and the wolves in the parish were wiped out, though some are said to have returned since he passed away.

Credits

A Book for Christmas: A Memory from Childhood: 'Julklapps-boken: Ett barndomsminne', from *1001 böcker för Sveriges ungdom: julklappsboken: ett barndomsminne*, ed. Helja Jacobson & Anna Landergren, 1933. Translated by Sarah Death.

The Legend of Saint Lucia's Day: 'Luciadagens legend', from *Troll och människor*, 1921. Translated by Linda Schenck.

The Princess of Babylon: 'Prinsessan av Babylonien', from *Troll och människor II*, 1921. Translated by Peter Graves.

The Rat Trap: 'Råttfällan', from *Höst*, 1933. Translated by Linda Schenck.

In Nazareth: 'In Nazareth', from *Kristuslegender*, 1904. Translated by Peter Graves.

Redbreast: 'Fågel rödbröst', from *Kristuslegender*, 1904. Translated by Sarah Death.

The Skull: 'Dödskallen', from *Troll och människor II*, 1921. Translated by Sarah Death.

The Animals' New Year's Night: 'Djurens nyårsnatt', from *Nils Holgerssons underbara resa genom Sverige II*, 1907. Translated by Peter Graves.